THE AMAZON INFLUENCE

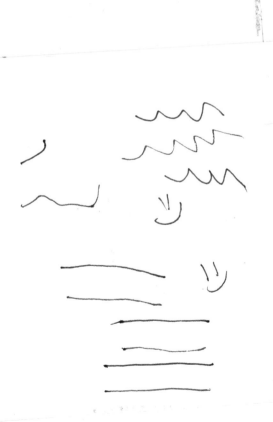

THE AMAZON INFLUENCE

Marion Woodson

Orca Book Publishers

Canadian Cataloguing in Publication Data
    Woodson, Marion.
    The Amazon influence

    ISBN 1-55143-011-8
    1. Title.
PS8595.O653A74 1994   jC813'.54   C94-910023-4
PZ7.W66Am 1994

Publication assistance provided by The Canada Council

Cover illustration and design by Carl Coger

Printed and bound in Canada

Orca Book Publishers
PO Box 5626, Station B
Victoria, BC Canada
V8R 6S4

Orca Book Publishers
#3028, 1574 Gulf Road
Point Roberts, WA USA
98281

10 9 8 7 6 5 4 3 2 1

For My Grandsons:
Charles, Thomas, Sam, Alec and Jake

To Ann Featherstone
for diligent, thoughtful, and creative editing
thank you

M.W.

Chapter 1

Sometimes Nick was proud of his mother. Sometimes he couldn't stand her. He was proud of her occupation. She was a marine biologist at the Pacific Biological Station in Nanaimo, and some people called her "Doctor." She was pretty famous and smart about anything to do with jellyfish.

But he couldn't stand her that morning — the day the loggers tried to start cutting trees on Gabriola Island. There she was, glaring at a bulldozer like a sea urchin prickling its spines at a whale, and being the big cheese. Organizing. Telling everybody what to do, including him.

It would be all right if that girl wasn't watching. Or even if the girl couldn't tell that Patricia Price was his mother.

Fat chance. His mother was taking off her sweater. Calling to him. She *looked* like a health and fitness poster — slim and athletic, square shoulders, shining hair — too bad she had to act like such a nerd.

"Ni-ick. Would you just put this in the bag. And hand me my sunglasses, they're in the side pocket." She pointed to a backpack lying in the grass beside the road.

"Toss it," he said, trying to sound nonchalant. Geez! You'd think it was perfectly fine for a fourteen-year-old guy to run around doing dumb little things for his mother!

Men's voices could be heard now in the distance, joking and calling to each other. Even the seagulls and crows seemed to stop moving and listen as the sounds grew louder with the dull thud of heavy boots. Eight men wearing hard hats and carrying chainsaws marched into view along the newly cut logging road.

Nick's mother, along with fourteen other people — four men, seven women and three children — stood shoulder-to-shoulder blocking the way. Some of them held hand-lettered cardboard signs.

"Here they come. Remember now. Non-violent civil disobedience. The reasoned position." Patricia Price pushed her sunglasses into place on the bridge of her nose with one finger, placed the palms of her hands together in a prayer-like motion and held them against her mouth, the two thumbs supporting her chin. That meant she was concentrating. Being logical and sending clear messages were very important to her.

The girl stood on a knoll, with one hand on her hip and the other shading her eyes. She reminded Nick of a statue — freedom, or justice, or something, standing like that in her white shorts and yellow T-shirt. Her eyes were blue. He knew they were blue. He had seen her before.

Who is she? How old is she?

"Can we talk?" Patricia Price called.

"Sure. Let's talk. What you want to talk about?" yelled a logger.

"About cutting these trees." Nick's mother stepped forward and the others closed ranks behind her.

Nick moved back among the tall shrubs where he could see without being easily seen. Of course he agreed with his mother and her group, most of the time. Forests are important; we all need trees. And birds, like spotted owls and that other one, the marbled murrelet, deserve a place to nest and all that, but why did this have to happen here, with the girl watching?

He sneaked another look at her. She looked different today. Before, she was wearing blue jeans and gumboots and one of those big sweatshirts. Yellow and white stripes. And her hair was wet.

"The lady wants to talk." The logger turned to his buddies and waved his saw in the air.

Several loggers spoke at once.

"Tell you what. You come back at four-thirty, then we'll talk. Yeah . . . . You tell 'em Mike . . . . We got legal rights. Why don't you just bug off?"

They reminded Nick of soldiers, wearing blue jeans and bright plaid shirt uniforms, stomping along in a purposeful marching way, swinging their saws like weapons.

The group with Nick's mother was an army, too. A mismatched army of all shapes and sizes, wearing baseball caps and cut-offs and muscle shirts and long skirts and straw hats and hiking boots and waving signs in the air like matadors tempting a bull with red flags, except they were not prepared to dodge or run.

"We'd like to talk now, man. Before you start," one of the sign-wavers yelled.

"We got a job to do, buddy. Just move aside. Nice and reasonable like," a logger yelled back.

The girl is about thirteen, I bet, thought Nick.

I wish I had the nerve to saunter over there and . . . except all this yelling is just too weird.

"We work now, talk later," shouted a logger.

"Get real, why don'tcha?" yelled a young boy, about ten years old, who looked as though he might be at a game. Baseball, or hockey, maybe.

"They want *us* to get real," said an older logger with a grey stubble of beard. "Real people don't suck kids into this kind of thing."

"It's their future at stake though, ain't it, buddy?" yelled a demonstrator.

The loggers were walking more slowly, looking at each other, shrugging their shoulders, grimacing, rolling their eyes.

"You don't know real from your frigging hard hats," called a man who was standing directly behind Nick's mother.

"Bunch of bleeding hearts. Don't know what an honest day's work is."

"Yeah . . . right . . . you got it, Joe," the loggers' voices chorused.

"Forests belong to our children . . . Immoral . . . No right," yelled the protesters.

Nick could decipher only some words on the waving signs. The messages, painted in assorted colours on chunks cut from cardboard boxes, were not easy to read from a distance. NO . . . SAVE . . . WILDLIFE . . . FUTURE . . . FOREVER . . . . One sign was clear: BIG TREES NOT BIG STUMPS.

"Move it. We talked long enough." The loggers had stopped moving and stood at attention. The names on the chainsaws were clear and bold on the shining enamel surfaces: HUSQVARNA, STIHL, HOMELITE, PIONEER, JONSERED.

"We'll move. Soon as you leave," called one of the demonstrators.

"If you don't want to earn an honest buck, for Chrissake get out of the way for them that do." The loggers were starting to shuffle their feet, take small sideways steps.

The protesters turned to stare at each other, eyebrows raised, mouths open in disbelief. One man stepped forward with an angry jerk to stand beside Nick's mother. "Honest? Ha! Honest is a word you gotta helluva nerve using," he said.

The voices grew louder and angrier, a crow started to scold, seagulls screeched. Nick felt more and more as though it were all a dream, or a movie, or a television news clip about anti-logging demonstrations in the Clayoquot Sound, or the Carmanah Valley.

This could not be happening on this peaceful little island.

And the girl was gone.

Geez! I missed my chance again. So what's new? Woulda blushed and stuttered, anyway. Nick sighed.

Nick's mother had been standing silently, her hands at her sides. She raised them, palms up, and then dropped them. Her shoulders slumped. So much for being logical and sending clear messages, the gesture seemed to say.

And the girl was gone. He would never see her again, and if he did she would think he was a complete idiot, anyway.

But maybe if he left right away . . . .

Chapter 2

It was raining. That's why her hair was wet. Ferry. Rainy day. On the ferry a couple of weeks ago.

The Prices' Volvo was the last car to get on the *M.V. Quinsam*. The wind and rain swirled inside as Nick's younger brother opened the door. Nick got out of the car, lowered his head into the wind and almost collided with Max, one of the ferry workers.

"Dammit! Watch what you're doing, boy," he said.

The lounge felt extra warm that day. Newspapers rustled, people talked, a baby cried, children crawled over the seats.

The door jerked open and a boy carrying a Ninja Turtles knapsack stuck his head in. "There's a car falling off the ferry," he yelled. People streamed out the door.

There *was* a car falling off the ferry, all right. The Prices' old dark blue Volvo. It teetered on the edge of the deck. It strained against the chain barrier. Each roll of the ship in the rough water threatened to send it plunging into Northumberland Channel.

The rain and wind snarled and swirled and stung. The ferry crew yelled and ran. They got ropes and tied them to the front bumper. They pulled and panted, and finally the car moved forward onto the rolling deck.

Max lifted a wooden tire wedge by its chunk of old firehose handle and jammed it behind the back tire with his foot, kicking it hard several times. "This thing," kick, kick, "couldn't have been shoved in there proper."

"How could the car move? It was in Park and with the hand brake on," Patricia Price yelled into the wind.

"Lady, it's in Neutral and no hand brake," called Max.

"I never get out without putting it in Park," she retorted

indignantly. "Never." She stomped to the car as well as she could manage, since the heaving deck made stomping difficult. She jerked the door open and got in, hesitated, then slowly and deliberately moved the car's gearshift.

And the girl had been standing there, among all the other passengers, watching.

Nick's attention was jerked back to the warm summer day. Brilliant streaks of sunlight reflected from chrome moulding. A big logging truck with a blue and silver cab was parked near South Road, just a few feet from where he had left his bicycle.

McKeghnie Logging was printed in bold navy-blue letters across the truck door, and two painted thistles curled underneath the name. The cab looked like a face, making haughty smile-like flashes in the sunshine, the windshield-wiper eyebrows raised in disdain. Flat pasture land was dull and pale behind the silver sparkle, and grazing sheep were no more than fluffy blobs in the background.

Nick was beginning to feel like a bit of a traitor, leaving his mother in the thick of it like that, but she could look after herself, and anyway things seemed to be simmering down a little when he had hurried away. Not *really* to look for the girl. Just because he'd had enough.

The logging road smelled earthwormy and looked like the heavy black lines in a colouring book, except the colours were the same on both sides of it: every shade of green in a giant box of crayons, blended with brown and rust and beige. Highlighted against this dense blur were splashes and drips of pink and blue and yellow.

Yellow is the perfect colour for a T-shirt. Nick looked for the hidden colours — clusters of purple salal berries, a pale orange lily, dark crimson Oregon grape.

A girl with arms the colour of wheat.

He wished he could forget about the way he had blushed and stumbled around. Doing chores for his mother. Like a dummy.

How did she disappear so fast?

Nick picked up his bike and glanced at his watch. Only 9:20. Hard to believe that all that logging versus anti-logging commotion had been going on for less than an hour. He had promised his mother he would meet Jonathan at Camp Miriam after his swimming lesson, but he still had over an hour to spare. Jonathan was getting to be a pain in the butt these days. Now that he was almost eight, Jonathan thought he was one of the guys and he did not appreciate being watched over by his big brother. The feeling was mutual.

Nick got on his bike, coasted slowly down the short incline to where the logging road joined South Road and turned right. Trees whizzed by: arbutus, alder, spruce, pine, cedar, yew.

Nancy, Debbie, Michelle, Ashley. I wonder what her name is?

He turned off the paved road, pedalled hard up a steep rocky little hill, dropped his bike in the churchyard and moved slowly along a narrow path pinched between the forest and a barbed-wire fence. The branches of the fir trees met over his head. Their scent filled his nostrils. Needles cushioned the ground. It was like a cathedral. They knew what they were doing, those ancient people who crept through the woods to thank the gods and spend countless hours chipping images into the sandstone.

What would a Coast Salish guy do in those old days if he saw a girl he wanted to talk to? Sure as heck wouldn't bumble around like the tribal clown at a potlatch.

A small black-capped bird ran headfirst down a tree trunk in short bursts, pausing at intervals to look and peck. Nick stopped to watch. Was it a nuthatch or a brown creeper? Brown creepers climbed up tree trunks in their hunt for food, and nuthatches climbed down. Or was it the other way around?

He heard a rustle of leaves behind him and turned. It was her. Nick put his hand over his mouth. Geez! Staring at birds. She'd think he was absolutely nuts. But she hadn't seen him. She walked with her head down, kicking the faded brown maple leaves on the path.

"Ahem." Nick gave a little cough and she looked up, startled, and stopped in her tracks.

Her eyes *were* blue. Were they ever.

"Hi . . . ah . . . a nuthatch. I think." He pointed to the tree.

"Nut? Hatch?" She looked puzzled.

"Yeah. The bird. Nuthatch. Or brown creeper. One goes up. One goes down." Nick stared at the tree trunk hoping to make an upgoing or downgoing bird appear to prove his point, but no birds were to be seen.

"Oh. Up and down," she said, and smiled and nodded.

Up and down! Way to go, Nick. She must think you're a yo-yo.

"Somebody told me there are petroglyphs in here. Are there? Do you know?" She stopped beside him on the path and looked at him in a friendly, questioning way.

This was better. Now he could be an expert about something. "Yeah. I'll show you." He led the way, holding branches back for her to pass.

She stopped and clasped her hands together as they moved into the sunlit glade. "It's beautiful," she whispered.

So are you, he wanted to say. A single wild rosebush at least twelve feet wide grew in the centre of the clearing, and a profusion of plump rosehips were beginning to turn red in the sun. Several areas of brown sandstone, each about the size of a room, were exposed among patches of small shrubs, dry grass, wildflowers, moss and weeds.

"Look!" she exclaimed as she knelt on the stone. She traced the design with her finger.

"It's a killer whale," he said.

Well, obviously it's a killer whale.

"Look at this one. And this." She ran from one carved image to the next, kneeling at each one, tracing the outlines with her finger or brushing her hand gently over the grainy surfaces.

Nick wanted to talk to her about the petroglyphs. To

point to the tangle of trees and undergrowth surrounding the meadow and tell her about the way he imagined the Stone-Age carvers coming here. Moving out of the forest. Smiling to discover such perfectly flat stone. He wanted to ask her how she thought they ever managed to find it in the first place, this small clear area on top of a hill, just right for ancient rituals. He imagined himself, the fearless explorer, bushwhacking his way through the dense forest and discovering this plateau. Preferably with a blue-eyed girl standing in the middle of it.

The bird songs and the smell of sunshine on the grass and the glow of rosehips and the soft spongy feel of moss underfoot could have been exactly like this when the very first human beings came. Was it clear then, so you could see the stone right away, or did they have to roll back moss, the way anthropologists rolled it back just a few years before when they found the wonderful chipped images there?

He didn't tell her these things, but he did point out a salmon that could be seen only when you stood in one particular spot. She seemed impressed.

"What's your name?" she asked.

"Nicholas. Nick. What's yours?"

"Allison." It was a perfect name and Nick wanted to say it out loud, but he couldn't bring himself to do so.

"Aw, Nick, this is sweet. Look at the little heart-shaped face," she said, cupping her hands to make a border around it. "Wow! This one looks like a dragon," she said, extending her fingers in a claw-like gesture and grimacing. "Hey, Nick! Look at this, what is it supposed to be?"

"Yeah . . . . It does . . . . Don't know." He felt awkward and gangling and decidedly uncharming, but she didn't seem to notice.

Allison sat down on a patch of green-brown moss where three miniature fir trees were trying to get a start in life. "Aren't they unreal? The little trees?" she said.

Nick sat beside her, bent his knees, decided that didn't

look cool, stretched his legs out with his ankles crossed and leaned back on the palms of his hands.

It wasn't wheat. Her skin. It was the colour of those mushrooms — Morels. When they are new — pink and gold and . . . .

Allison leaned forward to touch a tiny blue flower, and her hair swung over her shoulder and brushed against Nick's arm. It felt cool and silky and alive. He wanted to hold his hand over the place where her hair had touched, to keep the cool silky feel of it from blowing away. His arm didn't feel cool. It felt warm. So did the rest of him. Warm and sort of . . . was *languid* the right word? He wished he could think of some way to get her hair to touch him again.

Nick had always considered the one-acre clearing where the petroglyphs had been carved an enchanted place, but today it seemed totally bewitching. He sat on the moss beside Allison, leaned as close to her as he dared without, he hoped, looking uncool and glanced sideways at her when she spoke.

"Do you live here? On the island?" she asked.

"Yeah."

"What's it like? Living here all the time? Is it nice?"

"No. Well, yeah. Sometimes."

"We're just staying for a month," she said. "In those cabins near the park. Where do you live?"

"Just past there. Taylor Bay."

Finally Nick got enough courage to ask a question of his own.

"What's your last name?"

"McKeghnie."

McKeghnie! Oh, no. Not McKeghnie. Not McKeghnie of McKeghnie Logging.

"Does your father . . . ? Is he . . . logging?"

She nodded. "And some creeps are giving him a hard time, too. Trying to stop him." She clenched her fists and turned to stare angrily at Nick. She seemed, suddenly, to recognize him. "That was you, wasn't it? You were there. You were the one standing in the bushes. With that black sweatshirt. And a baseball cap turned backwards." She sounded as though wearing a baseball cap backwards was about the equivalent of wearing paper rabbit ears made in kindergarten.

"Well, they won't scare him. Not my father. He's got the law behind him. He'll log. A few tree-huggers won't stop him." She clamped her jaw shut, her chin jutted forward and her eyes flashed as she jumped to her feet.

"What do you mean?" Nick's voice came out a lot higher-pitched than he intended, so he started over. "What do you mean, tree-huggers? We . . . I mean, they just want to make sure there's still a tree or two left. A hundred years from now. There won't be a world here . . . for logging or anything else, if people keep massacring the forests." Nick's voice sounded loud in the glade, even to himself.

"Massacring the forests? Massacring? The forests?" Allison stamped her foot, wheeled around and ran toward the path.

"Oh! You! You're a, a . . . a geek. You island people are a bunch of, of storks. Or whatever it is. You've got your head in the sand," she yelled over her shoulder.

"Hey!" Nick called to her.

She stopped but didn't turn.

"Don't you think we could just discuss it? You know. Like normal people?" He stood with an arm extended toward her, palm up.

She placed her clenched fists on her hips, turned for a brief second, tossed her head, stared at him and said, "So now I'm not normal!" She turned and ran.

Nick could see her flying hair and racing feet as she pounded out of sight among the trees. Oh, well. Good riddance, he thought. He had seen lots of better-looking girls than her. Lots. Smarter, too. Didn't even know the difference between a stork and an ostrich. She must be pretty thick not to understand about protecting the forests.

Chapter 3

In Nick's head, he and Allison had a pleasant but serious argument for the next half-hour as he rode his bicycle past the Taylor Bay turnoff and along Berry Point Road to meet Jonathan. He finally persuaded her to see his point of view. In his head.

Jonathan, as usual, did not want to do anything that Nick suggested.

"Get your bike," said Nick.

"No. I'm leaving it here." Sturdy was the word for Jonathan. He had a sturdy body, sturdy legs and a sturdy disposition, although Nick thought that stubborn would have been a better word to describe his little brother. Jonathan's hair was short and curly, his eyes were hazel and he had a round face and a full lower lip. No matter how he stomped around and tried to look angry, Jonathan always seemed to be putting on an act.

"You can't. How will you get it home?" said Nick impatiently.

"Mom can get it."

"Come on Jonathan! Why should Mom have to get it?"

"'Cause I don't feel like riding it. I'm tired." Jonathan sat on a log beside the parking lot and shook his head. "And my hair isn't dry." He scrubbed his fingers through his hair, which had shrunk into tight little curls.

Nick frowned. "It'll soon dry in the sun. Come on, smarten up. You have to go home one way or the other. Start walking or ride your bike."

Other children between the ages of seven and nine milled around and then got into waiting cars, jumped on bicycles or started down the road in small groups.

"Bye, Jon. See you on Wednesday." A little girl waved and smiled and Jonathan waved listlessly back.

"Want a ride home?" It was Jonathan's friend, Michael.

"Sure." Jonathan jumped to his feet.

"Jon, you can't," Nick said quickly. "You have to stay with me. Mom said." What Jonathan needed at that point was a good swift smack on the butt, but his mom did not believe in any hint of aggression or coercion when it came to child raising. Or anything else for that matter. Fine for her. Jonathan was pretty obedient when she talked to him, although the talking sometimes seemed to go on forever.

Jonathan slumped down on the log again. Nick sighed and sat down on the log with his chin in his hands.

"Why aren't we going?" asked Jonathan after a few seconds.

"We are. Soon as you smarten up."

Jonathan stood up, grumbled his way to his bicycle, got on with a snort and pedalled along the road as fast as he could go.

Uncle Hayloft was mowing his lawn. Nick could hear the echoing sputter and roar as he turned on to Decourcey Drive. Jonathan was ahead, just turning into their own driveway.

Decourcey Drive circled around a seventy-acre peninsula at the north end of the island. Winding dirt driveways disappeared into thick stands of trees on both sides of it, and the owners of the one- to two-acre properties must have had a contest to see who could have the most hidden cabin, or trailer, or home. Those on the road's outside perimeter were on the waterfront. Uncle Hayloft's little log cabin was on an inside lot, and he had not entered the "most-hidden" contest. His house was set only twenty feet back from the road.

Uncle Hayloft was not a real uncle, although he was a second cousin twice removed, or something. His father and Nick's grandmother had been brother and sister. His name wasn't really Hayloft, either. It was Haylett Dudley Haversham Croft — about the most ridiculous name ever. Just asking for trouble, his parents were, giving a kid a name like that. Even in the olden days.

He did look more like a hayloft every day, though. Uncle Hayloft was tall and broad and square. His bushy grey hair stuck out in all directions, and more spiky hairs grew out of his nose and ears and eyebrows. He talked a lot about his "top-notch barber" and how much money it cost to keep getting his beard "trimmed just so," but it didn't look "just so" to Nick. Most of the time it looked "just *not* so." Uncle Hay wore small square glasses, like barn windows, and moved in a jerky hay-pitching way.

Every time Nick imagined Uncle Haylett at work, he thought about what Jonathan had said once. "I bet he works in a hayloft and makes his subscriptions out of grass and weeds and dandelions."

"You mean prescriptions," Nick had corrected.

"Yeah. What I said," and Jonathan's chin had jutted out.

Haylett Croft was a pharmacist by profession, but he was more or less retired. He filled in as relief worker at the drugstore across the street from the ferry terminal in Nanaimo. He didn't mind bringing home prescriptions and other small sundry items, like toothpaste and deodorant, for people on the island. He always said, "No trouble." And it was no trouble for *him*. He either told them to meet him at the ferry, or, if they lived at the north end, volunteered to "have Nicholas just pop it off to you on his bike."

Apparently there was a "popping off" to be done today, because Uncle Hay was turning off the rusty old mower and waving to Nick. There was. A small white bag, stapled shut. Nick was careful not to ask how Uncle Haylett was feeling, but he heard anyway.

"Pop this off to the Pickerings'. On your bike." Uncle Hay rubbed his back and groaned. "Back acting up again . . . too old . . . on my feet all day . . . pushy people . . . shove you around . . . rich get richer . . . government don't give a working man a break . . . built this country . . . bare hands . . . not fair. Whole kit and caboodle . . . against old folks . . . treat us like sh . . . manure." He heaved a mighty sigh. "And I think I'll have to take the dog to the vet."

Uncle Haylett lived by himself, not counting his so-called pets, which all belonged in haylofts, too. His dog was grey and stiff and old, his cat was grey and grouchy and scratched the furniture, and his budgie bird was grey and young and stupid. The only sounds resembling words Nick had ever heard it make were "greedy gree."

Uncle Haylett's voice droned on while Nick thought about short shorts, a yellow T-shirt, long hair and slender wrists the colour of new mushrooms. His reverie was interrupted by a question hanging in the air.

"Pardon?" said Nick.

"I said — " Uncle Haylett looked at him with a puzzled frown " — can you take it straight away?"

"Oh, yeah. The prescription. No, I'll take it later. After Mom gets home. I have to stay with Jonathan." Nick made his getaway.

Thomas Turner's house was next door to Uncle Hay's, but set much further back in the forest, and Nick caught only a small glimpse of it before he turned and wheeled down his own driveway. Thomas Turner wrote murder mysteries and liked to act rather mysterious himself. He would never mow grass or prune vines or rake leaves, like Uncle Haylett seemed always to be doing.

The Prices' house faced into Taylor Bay, which was on the west-facing side of the isthmus that connected the peninsula to the rest of the island. There was a small patch of wild grass and weeds — which they mowed and called "the lawn" — between the house and the low bank leading down to the beach. A larger cleared area behind the house held a woodshed, a few raspberry canes, one apple tree and two raised garden boxes in which Nick's mother grew vegetables. Standing guard over the back yard, which in some ways was the front yard because you approached it first as you came down the winding driveway, was Buddy.

Buddy was a member of the family. They had all worked on making that scarecrow, and it was at least four years old. Each fall they took the clothes off the broom-stick-and-two-by-four body, and each spring found a new wardrobe for it. This year Buddy sported a pair of Nick's old grey sweatpants, a blue Hawaiian shirt with hula dancers on it that Jonathan had paid twenty cents for at a garage sale, a black felt hat with two tall eagle feathers (Nick had found the feathers under the eagle nesting tree at the back of the property) and a velvet vest, formerly part of their mother's wardrobe, that Jonathan had spotted in a box of clothing intended for the Salvation Army. Jona-than insisted that the vest had to be buttoned at all times. Sometimes Nick unbuttoned it, just to find out how long it would take Jonathan to remedy the situation. It didn't take long. Jonathan was intent on "keeping Buddy's hooler dancers warm."

Nick leaned his bike against the woodshed and stood quietly for several seconds. Was that thunder? It seemed to be coming from the south. He called, "Jonathan? What are you doing?"

Jonathan opened the door, waved a magazine at him, said, "Just reading" and closed the door again.

Nick moved to the corner of the house and looked across the bay. It was over five hundred metres to the op-posite shore, a good hard swim, there and back. But Nick was not thinking about swimming at the moment. There it was again — a deep rolling roar. Something moved on the beach on the other side. He strained his eyes to see.

Just a log salvage. An old black tugboat edged into view from behind the branches of a tree. He watched a log roll and bounce over the driftwood and smash into the water with a fountain of spray. Just the beachcomber pull-

ing a salvage log off the beach. *Why am I holding my breath?*
He breathed deeply as he turned. He stopped. What was
that rustling whipping noise?

Geez, Nick, you're really hearing things today.

But something was wrong. He caught a flash of red
out of the corner of his eye. The scarecrow was wearing
red. His mother's red silk scarf was twisted in a tight knot
around the stick-and-straw neck. The wired pine cone eyes
were bulging half out of the head, and his mother's hat, the
white cotton one she used for gardening, was set on the
straw hair at a jaunty angle. It looked grotesque. Like a
strangled person.

Buddy didn't look like Buddy anymore. It looked
like . . . for a split second Nick thought it looked like Patricia Price in a strange distorted kind of way — wearing her
scarf and her hat, and her earrings. Big gold hoops with
pearls dangling from them hung on spikes of straw at both
sides of the head. Nick squeezed his eyes shut, shuddered
and looked around. Mom wouldn't have put her own
clothes on Buddy.

The yard was peaceful. Treetops swayed, and two
white blouses and some underwear fluttered on the
clothesline. He could hear the muffled putt of the tug's
motor and faint shouts of children's laughter in the distance. A loud screeching squawk pierced the air. The noise
was familiar, but he jumped. A blue heron laboured over
the rooftop, barely keeping itself airborne. Its skinny
stretched neck and spindly legs looked like they belonged
on a skeleton.

Nick shook his shoulders, squared them and flexed his
knees, willing them to feel normal. His hands shook as he
untied the scarf and took off the hat and earrings. Must be
kids, practising for Halloween. He poked the left eye back
into place, but the right one wouldn't stay where it belonged. He twisted and shoved at the wire and the pine
cone crumbled. Buddy's face had always made Nick think

of a little boy trying not to laugh when adults were being very serious about something — how to trap slugs with saucers of beer, for instance. Now, with one eye conical and brown and the other flat and whitish, it looked half-blind. Its aluminum-foil smile seemed about to change into a sneer, or a snarl.

How did kids get my mother's stuff?

What would Dad do?

Nick found Buddy's hat with the two eagle feathers beside a tomato plant in the garden and put it back where it belonged. He pulled it down over the straw face, almost covering the missing eye. That was better. Dad would be calm. He probably wouldn't do anything at all, so as not to scare Mom. Or else make a joke of it.

Nick opened the back door. He was in a hurry to get the hat, scarf and earrings back where they belonged before his mother came home, but Jonathan was feeling chatty.

"Hiya, Nick. Whatcha been doing? What's in that white bag in your pocket?" Jonathan was lying on his stomach on the couch, making swimming motions with one arm.

"A prescription. I have to take it to Pickerings', soon as Mom gets back." Nick hung the hat on a peg beside the door.

"Whatcha doing with Mom's scarf?"

"Just putting it away. She must have dropped it." He hurried into his mother's bedroom, but Jonathan followed.

"I can float on my back, and the teacher said I was goodest at dog paddles."

"Good, Jon." Nick unobtrusively dropped the earrings into the open jewellery box on his mother's dressing table.

"Can I have a cookie? I'm so hungry I could eat a elephant."

"I don't think so. Not until after lunch." Nick slipped the scarf over a rack in her closet just as they heard a car coming down the driveway.

"Aw, can't I have a cookie?"

"I don't think so. Ask Mom. I'm out of here." Nick headed for the door.

Nick's mother was on the telephone talking about logging when Nick arrived home from delivering the Pickerings' prescription. She used words like *genetic diversity*, and *ecological niches*, and *sympathetic media*, and *non-violent civil disobedience.*

"We've asked for a moratorium, but they'll probably try to get an injunction. Anyway, they've stopped for the time being," she said.

She talked like that for the next twenty minutes.

"I'm hungry. We ever going to eat around here?" said Jonathan. He carried a *Mad* magazine in one hand and a half-eaten apple in the other. "What are dog days?"

"Nick, will you make the salad?" His mother switched the phone to her right ear and called over her shoulder. "And ask Jonnie to set the table."

"What are dog days?" Jonathan flipped the magazine toward Nick and pointed at the back cover.

"You're supposed to be setting the table," said Nick.

"But what are dog days?"

Nick shook his head. "If you aren't old enough to understand, don't read it. Set the table." He shook lettuce leaves impatiently, and drops of water splashed onto the windowpane above the sink.

Jonathan stepped closer to Nick, tilted his head back and gave his brother one of his stare-them-down looks. "Come on, tell me."

"Boy! Are you ever going to grow up? You'll still be asking dumb questions when you're seventy years old." Nick leaned over and widened his eyes in imitation of Jonathan.

"Oh, sure. Mister Perfect." Jonathan wiggled his fingers near his face and smirked. "You knew everything in the whole world when you were seven. Even seven months . . . seven weeks . . . seven days . . . seven hours . . .

seven seconds . . . ." Jonathan's voice got higher and shriller. "Besides, Mister Smartass, I'm going to be eight years old pretty soon, anyway."

"Jonathan." Patricia turned her head and held the phone against her chest. "I heard that. And when I'm talking on the telephone and you speak in that loud voice I feel annoyed. I'd like you to set the table."

Geez! Her and her "I" messages. Ever since she had taken Communications Training she had been trying to teach them about "I" messages.

I wish I had the nerve to send a couple of "I" messages to that girl. I could wait outside the cabins where she's staying and talk to her. Forget about logging and stuff. Let the old people worry about that.

When you stand there with your hair blowing in the wind I feel . . . . Gulp. I feel like . . . I'd like to dive off a cliff and bring you a pearl. Or touch your hand. Or skateboard across the Strait of Georgia. Or hang glide to Mexico.

That afternoon they picked wild blackberries for the freezer. Nick was not crazy about blackberry picking, but there were worse jobs. The evening was spent answering Jonathan's *Mad* questions, or so it seemed.

"What's classic junk? How do you paint the town purple? What's a dork?"

It was ten o'clock before they remembered they hadn't picked up the mail.

"I'll go get it," said Jonathan as he dropped the magazine to the floor and scrambled to his feet.

"I don't like the idea of you going out alone this late. Anyway, it's past your bath time," said his mother. "Nick, would you mind?"

Nick didn't mind. The sweet smell of the nicotiana his mother had planted beside the back door followed him up the driveway. He frequently felt as though his arms were too long and his hands were too big and his feet were too far away from his brain. He wished his body would come together — be neat and compact and perform like a well-oiled machine. He was tall, just a shade under five feet eleven, and he weighed one hundred and thirty-eight pounds — so although he tried to think of himself as lean and muscular, he knew that some people would definitely call him skinny.

If sturdy was the word for Jonathan, then striving was the word for Nick. He always seemed to be striving to catch up to himself. To act more debonair and sophisticated, the way he looked. His hair was black, his eyes were very dark and deep-set, his eyebrows were thick and long — they almost reached the hairline at his temples — and his face was narrow and serious-looking.

He took his time as he walked along the road to the mailbox. One small light burned in Uncle Hayloft's house and Nick could see the grouchy grey cat sitting on the back of the couch against the window. That couch was the ugliest piece of furniture in the world, even without counting the torn and frayed places where the cat had scratched it. It was bright green and yellow. The room's decor was not green and yellow. In fact it was hard to tell what colour predominated. Haylett Croft was very fond of getting things for nothing, or buying things very cheaply, and his house and garage and yard reflected his habits. Nick considered throwing pebbles at the window where the cat was sitting.

He practised being a well-oiled machine and imagined he was dancing with the girl. No, not dancing. His feet could never get messages from his brain fast enough for that, and his hands started to perspire at the very idea of touching her. But you don't have to touch your partner, and you don't have to move your feet much.

The trees were dark against the sky and the air was still and warm. Black shapes swooped silently overhead and Nick slowed his step to look at the moon. To see a bat fly directly across the moon, he had decided at the age of six, would mean good luck by the barrelful. The bats refused to line up with the moon, so probably seeing three all at one time would do just as well. And he did see three at once, but hoped he would never have to prove it. Those things were faster than a speeding bullet.

He threw his head back, breathed deeply, swung his arms high and kicked backward with one foot on every third step. Not exactly dancing, but useful rhythm practise, he was sure.

I'll find out more about her. She's staying at those cabins, so I'll just hang around and, and . . . save her from drowning, or something.

He pulled the mail out of the box and saw a foreign stamp on a battered-looking envelope addressed to him. A letter from Brazil!

Chapter 4

A letter from Dad! How many lists in this one? Nick smiled to himself as he flopped onto the couch. He looked at the photograph on the bookcase. There they were, the whole family. Mom and Jonathan with their curly sable-coloured hair, golden flecked eyes and laughing upturned mouths. His father — tall, lean, dark-skinned, dark-haired, black-eyed, with a long narrow face.

"Always was a sober-sides," said Grandma and the old aunts whenever they spoke about Jim Price. But when Dad smiled, it was better than a straight "A" report card, brand-new roller blades and pizza with double everything. When Jim Price smiled, the world was in tune. Nick hoped that, since he had inherited his father's black hair, and dark brown eyes, and sombre long-faced look, he had also been blessed with that smile, but he was not sure that he had been. The old aunts said of Jonathan that handsome is as handsome does, but that Nicholas was a different sort — the dead spit of his father, and like him, too, in other ways: "Still waters run deep," they said.

Nick liked the idea of deep-running still waters and thought someday he might change his name to Nicholas James Stillwaters Price.

Nick's father was the only one in the photograph who was not looking at the camera. He was probably thinking about lists. As long as Nick could remember, his father had been a list-maker. He carried index cards in his shirt pockets and made lists — of things to do, things to think about, books to read, people to talk to, seeds to plant, you name it. Nick had been delighted when, at the age of ten, he had found the perfect birthday gift for his father: *The Book of Lists*.

It was mostly lists that were responsible for his parents' divorce two years earlier. He was pretty sure of that.

"Whenever I try to talk about feelings, what both of our needs are in this relationship, you, you . . . start making lists," Nick had overheard his mother say. Her voice was low and the way she hissed the s's in *lists* made him think about angry bees.

"But I have to make lists, so I'll remember what's most important to you," his father had replied in his "there, there, everything will be all right" voice.

"Your lists are escapism, that's what those lists are. Avoiding, that's what you're doing. Avoiding the issues. An avoidance mechanism." Her voice had changed from an angry buzz to a flat, tired drone and that's when Nick knew that everything was not all right.

Six months later they were divorced. A year after that his father was in Brazil studying the Amazon rainforests. He wrote to his sons every week, alternating turns. Nick liked it this way. His letters were his own.

There were lists, all right.

Dear Nicholas:

These are the things I have seen during the past week:

- *A river that carries the largest volume of water and harbours the greatest variety of fishes of any in the world*
- *A jungle so dense and teeming that not all of the scientists on earth could describe all its life forms*
- *A feather-duster worm*
- *12,000 square miles of Brazilian rainforest reduced to ashes from last year's annual burning for farms and cattle ranches*
- *A flock of flaming scarlet ibises*
- *The biggest butterflies in the world*
- *People and livestock living on rafts. The cows will*

plunge into the water for tufts of grass then swim to
floating corrals
– Llama herds with bright red tassels fastened to their ears
– A pink dolphin
– A fish with red scales. The scales are dried and used
as nail files
– Almost forgot stink bugs. How could one forget stink bugs?

Nick closed his eyes and imagined this strange tropical
world. He could see a pink dolphin, giant butterflies, cows
diving off rafts. Can cows really dive? And what did a
feather-duster worm look like? He could see his father, squat-
ting over a campfire, moving shadows making his face look
darker and more intense than ever, as he wrote lists. And
surely lists were the perfect way to tell about the Amazon.
Surely his mother would see the advantage of lists when
she read the letter.

These are the things I have heard during the past week:
– The whine of several million mosquitoes
– Birds called oropenoolas that sound like running water
– Monkeys howling
– Giant waves called Pororoca (Big Roar) that come up
the Amazon River from the sea. They are 25 feet high
and come up the river 500 miles
– The endless one-note bullhorn music of the cowboys.
The herds of cattle will follow this tuneless song all day
– The rallying cry "Save the forests" from conser-
vationists, politicians, rock stars and seringueros
(rubber gatherers)
– Gunshot (once) during an angry confrontation
between farmers and rubber harvesters

Nick wished he could be there. To hear gurgling birds and
howling monkeys and roaring waves and Brazilian cowboy
music. And his father's voice. His low, comforting voice.

He took a very deep breath, squeezed his eyes hard to keep tears from coming and went back to the letter.

Things I have swallowed during the past week:

- *Several bugs, species unknown*
- *Potatoes. They grow many varieties here and I think we've tried them all and then some*
- *Iguana*
- *Turtle eggs*
- *Sweet boiled tea*
- *Tinned tuna*
- *Fresh lime dipped in sugar*
- *Chemically purified (???) water*

Things I have missed most during the past week:

- *You*
- *Jonathan*
- *A bed with sheets*
- *Newspapers*
- *Solitude*

The expedition is going well, although the conflict between the farmers and the rubber harvesters is a complex issue. The farmers have been slashing and burning the jungle for generations, to plant new crops, while the Indians harvest the rubber without harming the trees. Pretty obvious which is the better practice, but it's not easy to tell that to a dirt-poor farmer who is trying to feed a hungry family.

I think of you often. Hug your brother and say hello to your mother for me.

Even his sign-off was a list.

With love
Your father

James N. Price
Amazon Expedition
Canadian International Development Association
Rua Dr. Moreria
Manuas
Brazil

Why couldn't his mom see how good the lists were? She was sitting in an easy chair under a lamp, her feet up on a footstool, reading *Journal of Fisheries and Oceans*, and sipping a glass of sherry. There was a sad and lonely feeling in Nick's chest as he looked at her. She looked so . . . so . . . what did *Whistler's Mother* look like? No, she was old and in a rocking chair. The *Mona Lisa*? No, but Mom really was pretty good-looking, for a mother. Especially there, with the lamplight shining on her hair, and no worry wrinkles on her forehead.

"Want to read it, Mom?" Nick handed his letter over.

If only Dad wasn't a list-maker, or Mom was, maybe they'd still be together. I could show him the cave where the otter lives with her two babies and I'd listen as quiet as can be while he explains about how otters eat shellfish, shells and all, and how their digestive systems work and all that.

And we'd go kayaking together and I could do my share of the paddling. Dad could relax and I'd paddle him around to Connery Cove . . . . He quickly pushed away the image of a long lump hidden under a faded tarpaulin behind the woodshed. He didn't think he'd ever again be able to look at a two-person kayak without a tightening of his throat and a hard stinging behind his eyeballs.

Maybe I can say something, or write a note. Make Mom change her mind. Get him to come back. We could even go there.

Forget it, Nick. Remember the "I" message the last time you tried to get her to change her mind?

"Nick, when you talk to me about getting back together with your father, I feel very sad, and guilty, too," she had said. "But I know I have made the right decision for me, and I will not change that." Period. She had brushed her hand across his forehead and squeezed his shoulder and said "I love you," and Nick's hopes had collapsed back into a small hard seed.

At least it didn't sprout so often as it used to. He must remember to be on guard and take his grandmother's advice to count his blessings or the seed might get the better of him.

"He sounds fine," said Patricia as she handed the letter back.

"Yeah, fine." Nick didn't look up as he gave it to Jonathan.

"What means teeming? What does it mean, teeming?" asked Jonathan.

"Geez," said Nick. "I'll explain it to you in the morning." He held out his hand for the letter and took it into his bedroom.

"Good night," he called as he closed the door.

"You all right, Nick?" He heard his mother's voice.

"Fine. Fine. Just tired."

The Prices' house had a rather unusual floor plan. Nick's bedroom was right off the kitchen.

His great-great-grandfather, who had owned and operated his own tugboat business, bought twenty acres of waterfront property at Taylor Bay in 1915. He built a two-room holiday cabin with no electricity and an outdoor toilet. Nick liked the pictures in the old photograph album of summer fun on the island. Whiskered gentlemen pitching horseshoes, corseted ladies drinking lemonade, little boys in sailor suits and girls in white dresses and straw hats with socks and shoes off, hunting for seashells on the beach. Uncle Hayloft was in one of the pictures, a round-faced baby in a bonnet, being held up for the camera by a young woman wearing a silk blouse, a long skirt and pearls.

Although people didn't talk about it much, apparently there had been a family squabble over dividing the property when the old man died, and most of it had been sold. Nick's great-grandfather had managed to keep the two-acre plot the cabin was on. He built a bedroom on each end of the old structure, one which opened directly off the kitchen, and the other off the living room, and there were still family picnics on hot summer days.

When Nick's parents decided they would like to live there full time, they added a wing, transforming the old cabin into an L-shaped house. A third, larger bedroom; a bathroom and laundry room off a short hallway; a new roof and porch; a stone fireplace; an electric stove and fridge — Nick could still remember how they opened a bottle of champagne and planned an old-style family picnic, like the ones in the album, the day they moved in.

The picture of that picnic included two of Nick's grandmothers, one grandfather, three great-aunts and five second and third cousins of assorted ages. Jonathan, a round-faced baby in a sunsuit with a clown face on the front, was being held up for the camera by Patricia Price, who was wearing shorts and a halter top. Uncle Haylett wasn't in it.

Nick lay on his bed and thought about his father. Maybe what he missed most was the special walks. They hadn't seemed special at the time, just regular walks in the woods, but every time he went with his dad, they found things: a hummingbird's nest with two little white peppermint eggs in it; a raccoon asleep in the deepest branches of a fir tree; a scattering of trillium in a meadow of moss; a wild rhododendron bush; a just-born fawn struggling to make its legs behave; and fungi and anthills and cocoons by the dozen. Together they had tasted budding willow leaves and tree sap and the insides of fireweed stalks. They had listened to insect orchestras and crow conversations, and tried to describe the smell of the ocean. Fish, licorice, salt, honey, rotting leaves, cooked cabbage, ripe cantaloupe, spices, camphor, urine, sulphur, iodine. There was scarcely a smell they could name that didn't seem to be in there, somewhere.

I wonder if we thought of cough syrup?
Good night, Dad. I miss you.

Chapter 5

Nick awoke to the sound of foghorns answering each other across Georgia Strait. Heavy mist enveloped the landscape, erasing familiar trees and buildings. The unseen ocean lapped against the rocks beneath the fog, sounding like a ghostly percussion band tuning up. It seemed like a good day to do something comforting and familiar — a visit to the galleries around Malaspina Point. That would do it. Nick didn't know why the caves should be called galleries, but he did know that they had been carved out of the cliffside by centuries of wind and wave action; that the Indians had considered the place holy and had left their dead there long before the white people came; and that a Spanish explorer, named Galiano, had drawn a sketch of them in 1792. No wonder there was a mysterious feel to them, especially when they were curtained shut by the fog.

"I'm going to kayak around to Malaspina Galleries," he said after breakfast.

"Just don't lose sight of the shoreline then," warned his mother.

"Mother! I've been kayaking since I was five years old, remember?"

"I know." She smiled at him. "But when I think you could be in a dangerous situation, I feel anxious and protective."

Nick's breath caught in his throat as he walked to the woodshed for his kayak. Every bush and tree and clump of grass was festooned with spider webs. The fog had outlined each filament in silvery grey, creating delicate, perfectly designed patterns. It looked like the designs on seashells, sand dollars or the finely drawn sketches of jellyfish his mother made when she wrote magazine articles.

Two little puddles of water lay in the middle of the old tarpaulin where it covered the seats in the two-man kayak. Dad had taken him out in that kayak a million times. Before he could walk, even. His father's hands had tucked the tarpaulin in.

Nick's mood changed. Suddenly the webs looked different. Not at all like seashell designs, or pen-and-ink sketches of jellyfish. They looked like spider webs. Ordinary, everyday spider webs. Made by spiders. Traps for flies.

The woodshed was not really an enclosed building at all. It had a post at each corner, a sloping roof and half-walls on three sides, leaving open spaces all around the upper part.

Nick's own single kayak was leaning against the woodshed wall on the ocean side. He carried it and his paddle down the bank and set them on the sand, then shifted from one foot to the other as he shook his thongs into the space where the seat was. He rolled up his jeans, carried the boat into ankle-deep water, climbed in and pushed off with the paddle.

Nick liked the feeling of resistance against the paddle as he moved his arms. Up and forward, down and back. The simple movements gave him a powerful feeling as the little boat skimmed through the water. Dip, pull. Dip, pull. Nick loved the ocean in the fog. He had never been afraid, although he had heard stories often enough about disasters at sea on foggy days. When he was out on the bay with the soft whiteness all around, the only sounds those of the paddle and his own breathing, he imagined himself grown up — a scientist, maybe a marine biologist like his mother, but more likely a botanist like his dad.

Then he began to think about another meeting with Allison. If there ever was another meeting. And *if* she wasn't still mad at him. Holding him personally responsible for the whole anti-logging thing. Maybe he could suggest that they agree to a moratorium between the two of them. Forget the whole issue, just for the summer, maybe, or . . . . No, probably he should try to be the strong silent type, because it was mostly when he had to move or talk that he blushed and felt awkward and shy.

He kept the faint outlines of trees and buildings in sight as he glided around the shoreline, stopping from time to time to drift and listen to the quietness and smell the fog-diluted brine of the sea.

He left the kayak on the beach in the little bay beside the galleries. The tide was going out, so the boat wouldn't be swept away, and there was no sense having to carry it further then necessary to relaunch it.

Nick looked toward Newcastle Island. It was only a few miles away in Georgia Strait and usually blotted out part of the view of Nanaimo, but there wasn't a view of anything today. No island, no trees, no beaches. Just a blank white wall of fog.

The craggy roof shared by the long line of caves hung in the mist like surreal sculpture. Visitors often stopped to ask directions to Malaspina Galleries expecting to see art, not caves. Nick liked caves better. He climbed the uneven ledge of rock.

"Grrr. Grrr."

The sound was like a miniature polar bear — or a raccoon. But a raccoon didn't snarl and growl unless cornered.

A small white dog was standing guard at the narrow ledge of rock where the caves began, trying hard to look fierce. Its bright black eyes and sharp little teeth made Nick laugh out loud, because it couldn't seem to keep its tail from wagging.

"What are you doing here? Are you lost?"

The dog scampered away and Nick followed.

A bundle of clothing appeared out of the mist against the farthest wall of the biggest cave. A dull khaki-coloured sweater, dark brown corduroy pants, a big loosely knit black toque, gumboots and, inside, a person. Two hands around two bent knees. The bundle seemed to be crying. The sweater heaved; there was a muffled sob. Nick stopped.

Another meeting with Allison McKeghnie? Omigosh! This was not the way it should happen. Not at all. Anyway, what would be the point of trying to talk to her? She thought all islanders were ostriches. No, storks.

She raised a teary face, stared at him for a few seconds, and lowered her head into her arms again. "Take a hike," she sobbed.

Nick turned on his heels and walked quickly along the cave floor toward the far end, his chin up.

Wait a minute. She doesn't own these caves. They're more mine than hers.

He turned and sauntered back, examining the graffiti on the wall. His own initials were there: *N.J.P. 1985,* right beside two intertwined hearts and the words *Allison loves Nick.* ALLISON LOVES NICK?

You're crazy. It says Allan loves Nicole. You know that. Seen it thousands of times. Those hearts were there even before N.J.P. 1985.

Nick was no longer proud of having his initials on the side of the cave, but in 1985 he had been only six years old and Uncle Hayloft thought it was a great idea.

"Fifty years from now, you come here. See them. I'll be six feet under. Remember your old uncle. Helped you paint your initials on the Malasapina Galleries." Uncle Hay always added an extra "a" to Malaspina.

Paint protected the sandstone surface from erosion so that the older initials and dates and messages of love stood out in bas-relief, but Nick wished he could make them all go away. Why should a cave look like a three-dimensional billboard?

Slivers of light glimmered overhead and Nick looked up. He smiled to himself. A spider web at least three feet wide stretched across the rock ceiling from the back of the cave to a small knob of stone on the open side. Beautiful was the only word for it. Some perfectionist spider had built that one. Perfect pattern, perfect spacing, perfect delicate movement in the fog-threaded air.

I have to show it to her.

Before he had time to think, he was standing in front of Allison.

"Come here. I want to show you something."

She looked up at him, glared, sniffled, pulled a wad of tissue out of her pocket and blew her nose, hard. She turned her head away.

"What's the matter?"

No answer, just a lift of the chin and a stare at the dog. "Go away."

"No. I'm not going anywhere until you tell me what's the matter."

I can be just as stubborn as you can. Nick squared his shoulders and felt tall and . . . what was that saying? About an immovable object and an irresistible force? He decided to be an irresistible force, or give it a good shot. Just for once in his life. "Come on. At least if you don't want to tell me what's the matter, at least let's talk. About something. Know what happens when an irresistible force meets an immovable object?"

Allison looked at him with, maybe, just a hint of a smile.

"Come on. I want to show you something." He reached for her hand and almost fell over backward when she actually gave him her hand and let him help her up.

"Thanks." She snatched her hand away. "Now just go away and leave me alone." Even with her eyes all red and her face streaked and swollen with tears, she looked like a person who meant what she was saying.

The irresistible force almost gave up. Almost. Nick would never know why he didn't blush and stutter and mumble and turn on his heels and stumble away. For once in his life he knew what he wanted. He wanted to be friends. To have Allison chatter and laugh and trust him. Even if her father was a logger.

He showed her the giant cobweb.

"It's nice," she said listlessly. "I'm going home."

"Do you have to?"

She nodded with her head lowered, turned and plodded away.

"Be careful," called Nick.

She stopped. "Huh?"

"Be careful. It's kind of narrow there. Don't step near the edge. It's not solid underneath."

"It looks solid." Allison leaned out over the water and tried to peer under the jutting rock she was standing on.

"Well, it's not." Nick made a lunge, grabbed her arm and pulled her back from the edge. "Besides, gumboots aren't too good for slippery places."

She stumbled against him, and he put his arm around her waist for a split second before she jerked away.

"Thanks," she said, but she didn't sound very appreciative.

"Okay. I just, just, don't . . . don't want you to get hurt," he blurted.

She looked directly at him for the first time and he blushed and looked away.

"But it's all right if my father gets hurt?" Her voice sounded angry and Nick turned back to face her.

"Whadd'ya mean?"

"Oh! Everybody . . . treats my father like a . . . a criminal." Her voice shook and her eyes filled with tears again. She fumbled for her soggy wad of tissue.

"I don't treat your father like a criminal," Nick said indignantly. "I've never even met your father, so don't blame me for everything."

Concentrate on communications training. My mother is smart about some things. Allison said something about her father. Active listening, that's it.

"You said people are treating your father bad?" That was the first cardinal rule of active listening, he remembered that much. Let the other person know you really heard what he or she said. He looked at Allison's face.

"Somebody tied wire around in the trees. He tripped and broke his wrist." Her face was angrier than ever. Her eyebrows scrunched toward each other, making deep furrows on the bridge of her nose. Her lips clamped shut in a tight straight line.

"Oh, no. I'm sorry."

"Sure you are!" She started to cry again in earnest.

He wished he could whip out a spotless white handkerchief and offer it to her, but he didn't have one. All he had in his pocket was a piece of an old towel that he carried to dry his hands on. He didn't like to paddle with wet hands.

"I . . . don't have a handkerchief, but would you like this?" He had it out of his pocket and was offering it to her. Dumb move. It looked grey and stained and yucky in the light of day.

Allison stared at it.

"It's clean. It's washed." Nick nodded his head a couple of times. "It's just old, and . . . ."

Allison started to giggle and took the torn piece of towelling and wiped her eyes and blew her nose and shoved it in her pocket.

"Allison. I really am sorry." He leaned closer and looked into her eyes. Allison took a deep breath, pulled the piece of towelling back out of her pocket, and twisted it. "I really am sorry," Nick continued. "That's no joke, a broken wrist. And stringing wire in the forests is bad. Very bad. I don't know who would do that."

"People who want to stop the logging, obviously."

"Maybe not." Nick shook his head vehemently. "I know my mother and her friends would never, ever do a thing like that."

"Well somebody did it." She stamped her foot in its big rubber boot with a soft thlump.

"I guess. So your dad must be pretty mad. You too."

"I'd give anything to find out who did such a rotten,

dirty, lowdown trick." She strangled the piece of towelling between her clenched fists.

"Maybe we can find out."

"Huh?" She looked at him with raised eyebrows.

"Maybe we can find out who did it. Between the two of us. You and me. We could ask questions. Sleuth around a bit."

"Why?" She looked suspicious.

"Well, so, so . . . so bad things will stop happening," said Nick.

"No. I mean why do you want to help? It's not your father who got hurt."

Nick picked up a piece of broken sandstone and threw it into the ocean with an angry swoop of his arm. "Listen! I don't like it any more than you do when criminal-type stuff gets started. Somebody could get killed."

The dog ran to Allison and stood close to her, ears cocked, neck hairs bristling. She had been standing with her shoulders slumped, arms at her sides, swinging the ragged piece of towel slowly back and forth in her right hand. She straightened her shoulders and clasped her hands together. "You think so? I mean, you think we really could find out something? Just us? They already got the police working on it. It's against the law, you know. Stringing wire."

"I know. I know. 'Course it's against the law. It's dangerous. Very." Nick felt a little surge of hope as Allison looked at him. "Come on. It's worth a try," he said.

"I guess."

"Come on. Let's walk on the beach. And make a plan."

Allison bent down to pat the dog. "Want to go for a walk on the beach, Missy?" Missy did, judging from her attempts to turn herself inside out in response to Allison's attention. "Missy wants to go," said Allison and looked at Nick with a small nod.

He offered her his hand as they scrambled down the ledge of rock that led around the point into Taylor Bay. Holding her hand made him feel light and surefooted.

Nick and Allison walked, climbed over driftwood, poked under seaweed and gazed into tidal pools in the quiet fog. Allison stooped to pick up pieces of sand-worn beach glass. Soon Nick was hunting for glass, too. She held them up and looked through them and exclaimed about the pale lilac ones being almost impossible to find, and the turquoise ones being a different shade of turquoise than any she had ever seen before, and the dark olive-black ones being from bottles hundreds of years old.

She took off her toque and shoved it in her pocket and her hair tumbled down and she combed it with her fingers.

It seemed that Missy must like beach walks that were on sandy, level beaches, and didn't care much for this one. The dog complained often beside the piles of driftwood they clambered over, and Nick kept going back to help.

He didn't feel at all awkward and shy in the fog on the beach with Allison. In fact, when he found an especially nice piece of beach glass and dropped it into her hand, he felt quite charming, like a knight in shining armour presenting his lady with a red rose. The fog had transformed him from a frog into a prince.

Nick was thinking about knights and ladies and roses as he bent and raked his fingers through a drift of loose sand behind a patch of seagrass. Bits of shell and glass, tiny pieces of twigs and worn and soggy pine cones stirred to the top. His hand touched something solid and he scribbled around it with one finger. It was straight and slender. He leaned down and saw a very small rose, stamped into dull grey metal.

"Allison, look," he called.

"Oh, Nick. It's neat. It looks really old." She knelt beside him and they scooped sand away. Their hands touched often, not always by accident. At last they saw the bowl of a spoon wedged into a crack in the stone. Very gently Nick moved it in one direction, then another. It came free and he handed it to her.

"An old spoon. A really old spoon." Allison's lips were slightly parted and her eyes looked shadowy as she held it cradled in both hands. "With a rose on it. It's beautiful. Just beautiful." She looked at Nick with a small smile. "Is it silver?" She turned it over and peered at it closely.

Her hair spilled forward and Nick reached to touch it, then snatched his hand away and stepped close to her. He leaned over the spoon, pretending to be looking for some markings on it. Her hair touched his cheek. It sent the same cool-warm feeling through him as at the petroglyphs, but now he was sure that languid was not the right word for it. He didn't know what the right word was. Maybe sensitive . . . sensitized . . . . No. Sense something. Sensual. That was it.

"Or pewter," he said, and his voice cracked. He cleared his throat. "It could be pewter." That was better. He sounded pretty matter-of-fact.

"I wonder how it got here? How old do you think it is? Maybe the Spaniards lost it. Or Captain Vancouver when he was messing around here, circum . . . circum . . . what?"

"Navigating. Circumnavigating," said Nick.

She nodded. "Yeah. Circumnavigating. How could we find out? Maybe, maybe it's from a shipwreck, or . . . ." Allison's face had lost its dreamy look and was sparkling with animation. "Here." She offered him the spoon. "I bet your mother will like it."

"No. You keep it." Nick lightly pushed her hand away.

"No-no-no-no. You found it. It's yours."

"Allison, I want you to keep it. Just for, for, a souvenir." Before he knew how it had happened, he was holding her hand over the spoon with both of his own and looking into her eyes.

"But maybe, you know . . . sometimes you give things away. And then, like after, you know, you wish you still had it? The thing you gave away? Like when people break up and stuff."

Break up? When people break up? Does that mean she thinks we could get to be a . . . a couple . . . who could break up? Naw. Nick felt like singing and shouting and leaping into the air.

"I want you to keep it." He dropped her hands and turned away so she wouldn't see him blush. "I won't be sorry. I promise," he said to Missy, who was sniffing and scratching under a log.

"Thanks, but . . . if you change your mind . . . . How can we find out about it? My mother knows a bit about old stuff. I think she's got a book. If it is really valuable, Nick, I'm giving it back."

"If it's really valuable, we'll sell it and split the money." The wind had cooled Nick's face and he turned back and spoke directly to her.

"I'm not selling my share. Never." Allison held the spoon against her chest. "If it's really valuable, I'll pay you half of what it's worth. Deal?"

"Deal," said Nick and they shook on it.

They sat on a log. Allison held the spoon in the palm of one hand and fingered the beach glass in her pocket with the other. The sound of waves washing on the beach was like soft music. The air felt moist and warm. Allison slipped the spoon into her pocket, put her elbows on her knees, her chin in her hands, and leaned forward. She looked worried again.

"What?" said Nick.

"Do you really think we could, Nick? Find out who did it?"

Nick shrugged. "We could sure try. Doesn't hurt to try."

"Let's try. We'll solve it ourselves. I'll be Sherlock Holmes and you be Watson." She grabbed her knees with both hands, pulled them up, leaned back and laughed. Her eyes sparkled. Nick thought she looked about as much like a pipe-smoking detective as Missy the dog looked like a bus driver. "Let's start right after lunch. But where do we start?"

"The scene of the crime, old fellow. The scene of the crime." Nick made his voice as deep and English-sounding as he could.

"Jolly good, old chap. Yes, by George, let's start this afternoon. At the scene of the crime. We'll meet . . . where's a good place?"

"Do you have a bike?"

She nodded.

"Bring it. I'll meet you by the big maples on Berry Point Road."

"Okay." She looked at him steadily with her blue eyes and he almost turned into a frog again. "And thanks," she said. "For cheering me up, and . . . ."

She gazed across the water where the treetops on Newcastle Island were floating up out of the thinning mist.

Chapter 6

By one o'clock in the afternoon, the fog had burned off. The island was itself again. Nick's kayak was back beside the woodshed wall, and he was heading for the mailbox. Thomas Turner and Uncle Hayloft were standing by the side of the road, talking.

Thomas Turner really did have an English accent. He wore tartan shirts and jackets with leather patches on the elbows. He smoked a pipe, had a neatly trimmed little mustache and said "jolly" and "by jove" and "old chap" and "sticky wicket." He wrote mystery novels and was a little strange. Well, not strange, exactly, just maybe like one of the characters in his books. Reclusive, preoccupied, solitary — an absent-minded professor type. And he was *always*, so the islanders said, looking for mysterious happenings — material for his books.

He was not looking for mysterious happenings at the moment, though. He seemed to be giving Uncle Haylett a shopping list. At least Nick wouldn't have to deliver it, since Thomas Turner and Uncle Haylett lived next door to each other.

"And some razor blades, and a packet of those good HB pencils, if you would be so kind, sir. Jolly good of you. Save a trip to the city. Extremely busy at this point in time. New novel hatching, don't you know." He scribbled on a little pad of paper, tore off a page and handed it to Haylett.

"Yup. Family owned this whole point. Whole damn thing." Uncle Haylett waved his arm around jerkily, like he was a referee making a call on a football field. "Over a thousand foot of waterfront. Look what I end up with. Would you believe it?" Uncle Hay's voice was loud as he glared at the ground and tugged at his beard.

But Thomas Turner wasn't listening. He murmured, "Thanks again, old chap," and walked back toward his own driveway. He stopped. "Oh, yes. The money, old friend. Shall I give it to you now?"

"Later. Later's fine. There's Nicholas. Nicholas, I need you for a minute."

Oh, no. Nick had been hoping he could get by without being needed for "a minute." He wished he could pretend that he hadn't heard, just keep on walking, but of course he couldn't. How could anybody not hear Uncle Haylett's deep raspy voice? Even if "a minute" really meant a minute, it wouldn't be so bad, but often Uncle Hay's minutes were pretty long and involved a lot of scrambling around: climbing trees to prune a particular twig, or climbing ladders to reach something from a high shelf, or climbing up on the roof to remove a fallen branch.

"Yeah? Can't stay long. Got a, an appointment."

"Won't take long. WD40. Top shelf."

"Which top shelf?" asked Nick.

In his house, carport and various and assorted sheds, Uncle Hay must have had at least eighteen top shelves, all crammed with junk.

"Inside. Oh, my aching back." He led the way, then stopped and turned to wave at the Prices' car scrunching past on the gravel road. "Where's your mother off to?" he asked.

"They're going to town. Groceries."

Come on, let's get on with it.

Uncle Haylett's house had just two rooms. The kitchen and living room were one large area, with a kitchen table and wooden chairs and fridge and stove at one end, and the couch and a couple of unmatched overstuffed chairs at the other. A small bedroom adjoined the living area.

"Which shelf?" Nick opened the screen door and looked hopefully at top shelves. Maybe he could see the oilcan from there. But he couldn't.

"There. Behind that electric knife." Uncle Haylett pointed and dragged a wooden chair across the floor, and Nick stood on it and lifted down the knife.

The grey budgie screeched and flapped around. Birdseed and feathers and scraps of newspaper along with other obnoxious bits and pieces clouded the air around the cage. It had learned a few more sounds, none of them at all pleasant or musical to Nick's ear. As well as "greedy gree" it now said things that sounded like "glwk, gwlk," and "crok, crok," and "gli, gli."

The grey cat awoke and stood in the middle of the couch, extended its claws and arched its back.

Thank goodness the WD40 had a little red siphon fastened to the tin with an elastic band. Nick spotted it and pulled it out from among a million other tins, bottles, jars and plastic containers, and handed it down.

The old grey dog had joined the party. It was standing in the doorway looking around, giving short husky barks and, it would seem, trying to decide whether or not to howl. It looked as though it did need a vet. Or vitamin pills. Or better yet, the Fountain of Youth.

Nick made it to the mailbox without any more interruptions. A little card told him there was a parcel to be picked up at the Post Office. Probably a birthday present for Jonathan. Dad always sent things good and early.

Allison rode her bike like Aphrodite riding a winged horse. Aphrodite didn't really ride Pegasus, but if she had, Nick was sure, she would have looked exactly like Allison. She was wearing a pink T-shirt and white short shorts, her hair was streaming out behind her, and her legs flashed in the sunlight.

The logging site looked different today. For one thing, there was no blue and silver truck parked on the road, and the road itself was drying out, turning grey and smelling of dust. The bulldozer was still there, parked in a shallow dip of underbrush.

On one side of the logging road grew thick tangled shrubs and small trees, with a cliff edge dropping into space thirty metres away. On the other side were tall trees.

"Let's go look at it. The ocean. Before we sleuth," said Allison. They stood, holding their bicycles, and looked down.

Connery Cove was at the foot of a high cliff, on the remote southwest side of Gabriola, looking toward Mudge Island. Dodd Narrows separated the two islands, and there the ocean roared, buckled and swirled in deep pools as too much water forced its way through too narrow a space. Because the water just below the cliff was close to the approach to the narrows, there was seldom much marine traffic there. It was dangerous to go through except at slack tide. But to the northwest, the distant scene from the clifftop would have made painters run for their easels. Vancouver Island mountains punctuated the horizon. Chugging tugs pulled barges, sailboats gathered the wind, quiet log booms floated along, and big ferries and fish trawlers bustled about their business.

The wild creatures were not afraid to live close to fast-running seas. Gulls, cormorants, ducks, seals and sea lions dived and swam and flew and perched below and around the cliff edge where Nick and Allison stood. They looked for several minutes without speaking.

"Better get on with it." Nick broke the silence and turned.

A large animal lifted its head and sniffed the air as Nick and Allison pushed their bicycles across the road into the edge of the forest and laid them on the ground. A deer. Allison stopped in her tracks and stood perfectly still, her eyes wide, her mouth slightly open. The deer walked slowly away, turning to look at them twice, before disappearing into a glade of thick underbrush.

"He is just, just the most beautiful thing," Allison whispered and let the air out of her lungs in one long breath.

"It's she," said Nick.

"Pardon?" The blue eyes were looking directly into his.

"It's 'she.' She's beautiful. It's a doe, because it doesn't have antlers."

"Eyes. The darkest brown I've ever seen." She leaned a little closer and partly closed her own eyes.

"Yeah. Deer do have nice eyes." Nick glanced away.

"Not the deer. Yours. They're the darkest brown."

Nick blushed, turned away and busied himself pushing bushes aside to make space for them to get to the deer path. "Now be careful. There might be wire anywhere. Do you know exactly where it was your father tripped?" he asked.

"No. Near the end of the road, across from the big old cedar tree is all I know."

They moved cautiously through the undergrowth, looking for wire. "How far up the tree would they tie it, do you think?" said Allison.

"Probably pretty close to the ground." Nick crouched as he walked.

"Listen. What was that?" Allison whispered.

"What?" Nick stood straight and was still.

"That. Listen. There. That noise."

Nick turned his head from side to side. He strained his ears. He could hear nothing but forest sounds. Birds chirruped and sang and whistled, insects buzzed and hummed and vibrated their wings, small animals rustled and pattered and squeaked.

Allison had moved close to him.

"Can't hear anything." He shook his head.

They both jumped at an explosion of sound. A great roar. A grinding crash. The ground shook. It sounded like . . . . He looked at Allison. "Sounds like the bulldozer."

She shook her head. Her eyes were wide. "No. The workmen have gone to town."

"Well that's what it is. A bulldozer."

"Sounds like it, but who . . . ?"

"We better find out." Nick started to scramble toward the sound.

"Maybe we should be careful." Allison looked pale and her hand was trembling as she touched his arm.

"Why? Somebody started it. Maybe the guy who set the wire?"

"No. Stop." Allison grabbed his arm with both of her hands. "I don't like it."

The noise changed — from loud to muffled, then loud, then muffled. There was the sound of cracking branches, as though a huge machine were tumbling down a steep cliffside. They crept carefully through the undergrowth, keeping low.

Nick stopped and raised his head, then crouched down and whispered, "I see the logging road. I think the sound is coming from over the other side of it."

"Be careful. Watch for wire, too." Allison's hair had fallen forward over her face, and she brushed it aside. It had twigs and leaves in it, and there was a long red scratch on her forearm. A yellowjacket buzzed around her head. She rolled her eyes and slapped at it with one hand.

"Try to ignore it. Move slowly," whispered Nick.

Finally they were at the edge of the road, near where the bulldozer had been parked.

"We'll make a dash for it. Across the road," murmured Nick.

"No. Somebody might see us." She grabbed her upper arms with her two hands and shivered.

"We gotta find out what happened. Smell." Nick sniffed. The smell of diesel fuel and exhaust hung in the air. "I'll go first, across to that bushy place. Then if nothing happens, you come over." Nick raised himself to a semi-crouching position, ready to run.

"Okay." But she didn't look as though she thought it was okay. She looked pale, and sweaty, and frightened.

"You okay?" he whispered.

She nodded. "Just go."

Nick went.

He ran, crashed into the bush and hunkered down. All

was quiet. Allison ran across and crouched beside him. Still quiet. She was looking a little better. The short run had put some colour back in her cheeks and she had smoothed her hair back.

They moved cautiously toward the noise. It was coming from below the cliff. A huge machine *had* tumbled down the steep cliffside. They crouched in the underbrush and stared at the ugly torn roots and dangling vines where the bulldozer had gone over the edge. Into Connery Cove, one hundred feet below.

"They'll never get it out of there," muttered Nick. The machine was still running, sounding faint and jerky. It coughed, sputtered and was quiet.

"What's that?" whispered Allison.

"Sounds like somebody running." Nick stood, then ducked again. "He's on the road. Be quiet," he warned. "He's coming this way."

They could hear branches snap and twigs crackle and the sound of panting as somebody rushed along the rough path the bulldozer had left, straight toward them.

They lay as flat as they could.

A man stopped and stared at the damaged cliff edge. He clenched his fists and stood with them on his hips, then turned on his heels and hurried away as noisily as he had arrived. They heard the sounds of his footsteps fade as he reached the logging road and raced down it.

There was a noise in the bush near them. Not a loud noise, but a different noise. A louder rustle. A low whistling sound, like someone drawing in a sudden breath. Nick's heart stopped beating. Was somebody there? They both turned their heads and were very still. A mosquito whined and landed on his forehead.

They had to do something. They couldn't stay here forever, lying on their stomachs on top of spiky salal, prickly Oregon grape and tickly wild grasses.

"We're getting out of here." Nick jumped up, grabbed

Allison's hand and pulled her along the bulldozer path, across the shallow ditch and onto the road. They raced for their bicycles.

Three hours later they were sitting on the Prices' front deck drinking lemonade.

Everybody on the island knew by now that McKeghnie's bulldozer had been sent crashing over a cliff into Connery Cove. And most of them were wondering if anybody would ever be able to get it out of there.

"It was a ferry worker who phoned my mom," said Allison. "To tell her to tell my dad about the bulldozer. I think his name was Mac." She twirled her glass and studied the swirling liquid inside it.

"Max?" asked Nick. "Was it Max?"

Allison nodded. "Yeah. That was it. Max."

"He's the one we saw. Running." Nick leaned back in his chair and took a gulp of lemonade. "He works on the ferries, directing traffic. Kinda grouchy guy."

"I thought you recognized him. So he's the guy we saw. Right after the crash." Allison fished a lemon seed out of her drink with her finger, and slid it up the inside of the glass.

"Funny," said Nick. "I wonder if Max could've done it himself. And then came running back. Just to check it out, you know. To make sure the job was done right."

"But he had already phoned the police when he talked to my mother. I wouldn't think he'd phone if he did it himself." Allison scrubbed at a berry stain on her shorts with one finger.

Nick shrugged. "It's hard to say."

"And what was that other noise? Like somebody taking a deep breath."

"Probably nothing. You hear funny noises in the woods all the time." Nick wished he felt as calm as he was trying to sound.

"One thing's for sure," said Allison. "Your mom will think the loggers did it, just to cause a real blowup. And my dad will think your mom's environment guys did it. It's all very depressing." She set her glass down and her head drooped.

"Then we have to find out who did it." Nick smacked his palms against his knees and leaned forward. "I'm going back there. To look for clues."

"Not without me, you're not," said Allison. She stood, squared her shoulders and gave Nick an I-dare-you-to-try-and-stop-me look.

Chapter 7

Two small groups of people were gathered on the cliff-side above Connery Cove to watch the salvage operation.

The loggers stood with arms crossed or hands in blue-jeans pockets, bright red and blue plaid shirtsleeves rolled up, heavy hobnail boots making patterns on the bent grass.

Some of Patricia Price's friends were standing close together, shaking their heads, talking to each other and pointing to the bulldozer tracks leading to the cliff edge.

Nick was standing by himself just apart from his mother's group. Jonathan had wanted to come, of course. Anything to do with large machines and crashes was pretty high on his list of favourite things to see. But his mother had said she'd rather he stay home with her and bake cookies. They could both hear about it later from Nick. Jonathan had resigned himself to her suggestions, after about twelve minutes of arguing.

Allison, too, had wanted to come. "But my mother said it would be too much for any of us," she told Nick. "To watch Dad trying to get the bulldozer out of there. Especially when it was deliberately caused by some weirdo," she added, with a toss of her head and a narrowing of her eyes.

The bulldozer lay tilted precariously on a pile of huge rocks. A barge was grounded in shallow water nearby. The figures scurrying back and forth on the beach below looked like Jonathan's micro-machines transformed into robots, the way the sun shone on their hard hats. One of the robot men climbed over the driftwood and rocks and pulled himself up onto the teetering bulldozer with one hand.

"By jingo. I wouldn't want to be in that bloke's shoes right now," said Thomas Turner, who was standing close to Nick.

A cheer went up from the crowd as the bulldozer shuddered and, several seconds later, the sound of a motor reached the clifftop.

"He'll never get it out of there," said one onlooker. He was wearing those mirror-type sunglasses, and they reflected everything in various shades of blue.

"If anybody can get that baby offa there, Scotty can do it," said one of the loggers, an older man. "McKeghnie's the best dozer man I ever seen. Even with a broken arm."

The watching crowd was silent as the machine inched forward. It was tipped at a crazy angle. Nick gasped as it lurched from one side to the other. It was a good thing Allison hadn't come. Like her mother had said, it would probably get her too upset.

"By jove, I believe he's going to do it," said Thomas Turner.

"Look, Jason," said a woman who was kneeling on the grass, holding a small child's hand and pointing. "See the big machine down there? Watch. Whoops! He almost tipped right over. See that? Isn't that exciting?"

The little boy was exclaiming and pointing to a flying seagull that was changing shape as it turned like a white flag in the wind.

"Give'er hell, Scotty. Atta boy!" called a young logger who was wearing blue jeans and a leather belt with a large buckle in the shape of a bucking horse.

Scotty gave "her" hell and the bulldozer crawled steadily over the driftwood and onto the barge.

"Well done! Well done!" yelled Thomas Turner, and clapped his hands, but not very loudly. One of them was holding his pipe. "Nature will complete the task. Good show."

Nature would complete the task, all right. Although the bulldozer weighed twenty-five tonnes, the incoming tide would float the barge off the sand so the waiting tug could tow it away to an accessible landing site.

Nick heard snatches of conversation as the loggers

stood together and talked in loud voices he suspected were meant to be overheard.

"Bloody machine is worth a quarter-million dollars . . . . "

"What scumbag would do a thing like that?"

"Maybe slow us down a bit, but sure as hell won't stop us."

His mother's friends looked worried and talked with anxious voices.

"Getting out of hand . . . ."

"Bad business."

"Never convince them it had nothing to do with us."

"Really too bad."

Nick saw Max. He was standing apart from the others, at the place where the bulldozer had been parked. He stood exactly as he had the day before, right after the crash — his clenched fists on his hips. He was chewing on his lower lip and frowning at the toe of his boot. He glanced up, caught Nick looking at him, tightened one corner of his mouth in a disgusted-looking way and lowered his head again.

Splintered trees and uprooted salal jumbled the path the bulldozer had followed just before it went over the bank. A snarl of blackberry vines dangled from a broken dogwood tree branch. Grass and buttercups were mashed together, jammed into deep pockmarks by the huge bulldozer lugs. And something else. A little patch of something, like paper, just showing under the dirt.

Nick looked around. Max had shoved his hands into his pockets and was walking away. Thomas Turner was moving absent-mindedly along the road, deep in thought. Others were turning to leave.

Nick scrabbled around the paper with a twig and pulled out a book. A whole book — muddy and stained, with some of its pages shrivelled and curled. He turned his back to the others, brushed the dirt off the book's cover and read the title. *Terror on the Island,* by Thomas Turner.

Could this be a clue? Didn't seem to make much sense as a clue. Still, it was at the scene of the crime. He walked to his bicycle, trying to hide the book as much as possible with his hand and look, at the same time, as though it were just something that he happened to be reading right now. He should show Allison. Even if it was a false lead, at least it was something. But nobody was home when he managed to screw up enough courage to knock on the door of cabin number seven on his way past the Taylor Bay Cottages.

Chapter 8

Nick checked on Buddy, as usual, when he got home from the bulldozer rescue. Buddy looked fine from a distance, except . . . .

Was it leaning backward a little more than usual?

He jumped off his bicycle and hurried over to get a closer look. The scarecrow was leaning backward, all right. One of Nick's mother's old purses had been taken out of the recycling box in the woodshed and hung over its shoulder. A dartboard was tied to its back with a piece of twine. In the bull's-eye, a dart was wedged right through the cork *into Buddy's heart.* A splotch of red paint looked like blood pooled on the board.

Come on, Nick, get real. We're talking scarecrow here. A scarecrow does not have a heart, or blood.

But why? What was the point of it all? Nick stood staring in disbelief. He shook himself, yanked the dart out, lifted the twine over Buddy's head and tossed the board behind the woodshed. He shoved the purse back into the box of stuff for the recycling depot and put the dart in a galvanized pail in the carport that held rusty old spikes and odds and ends.

Maybe I shouldn't have done that. Touched it. Maybe there could be fingerprints . . . . Should I call the police? Sure! I can hear it all now. "Oh really, Son? Now that's a pretty serious crime. A dartboard hung on a scarecrow, eh? We'll get right on to that one. You bet we will." Nick snorted to himself at the thought. It must be a joke.

He could smell chocolate chip cookies as he opened the back door. Patricia was humming as she dipped a fork into flour and pressed it into balls of cookie dough.

Jonathan sat at the kitchen table with a partly eaten cookie in one hand. "Hey, Nick. Did they get the bulldozer out? We got a parcel from Dad. Mine's straw. Yours is still wrapped up. Look!" He held a straw toy truck with its box filled with little straw people wearing scraps of bright cotton fabric for dresses and shawls and trousers and hats.

"Hello, Nick. How did the salvage operation go?" Their mother looked up.

"Better watch out, people," warned Jonathan. "You're going to crash right over the edge!" He pushed the straw truck up a Lego bridge and it tumbled off, scattering the brightly clothed straw people in all directions.

"Fine. They got it on the barge. Where's my present from Dad?"

"On your bed."

Nick sat on the edge of his bed and lifted the brown paper bundle out of a box. Rough hemp twine was tied tightly around it in six different places, so close together that you had to pull the knots aside to read the name and address. Trust Dad. He would put names and addresses on both packages, even though they were shipped together in a single box.

The twine was stubborn. It wouldn't slip over the edges, and the knots wouldn't untie. Nick snatched some nail clippers from his desk and clipped through twine, and twine, and more twine, until finally he was able to unwrap the coarse brown paper.

More red. Nick wished that it were some other colour. Green. Or blue. There was some green and a little patch of blue, but they didn't do much. Just sat there providing a nice neutral background for the red. Dark blood-coloured red. Ibis feathers? What was it?

It had a short handle woven of grass with a small egg-shaped figure made of stone attached to it with leather thongs. The stone had crudely carved features — round wide-open eyes and a rectangular gaping mouth. At the top of the stone face, providing a headdress, were feathers. Short blue and green ones formed the base for long soft red ones. The contrast between the grimacing face and the soft feather plumes made the whole thing seem startling. Like the difference between freshly baked chocolate chip cookies and a stabbed scarecrow.

There was a note:

Dear Nick:

I hunted high and low for this. I saw some Achuara Indians using similar instruments in ritualistic dances. According to local practice, a medicine stick has the following powers (when used by a qualified shaman, of course).

- *it can draw evil spirits away from sick people*
- *it can send messages to dead ancestors*
- *it can make a warrior fearless in battle*
- *it can identify a criminal and make him confess*
- *it can be used to cast a spell and even to cause death*

I wasn't able to learn as much as I'd like to know about how the spell-casting is done, but apparently victims show the following symptoms:

- *forgetfulness*
- *listlessness*
- *nausea*
- *double vision*
- *loss of appetite*
- *loss of muscle control*
- *eventual death unless more powerful magic can be found to counteract the spell*

I will find out more about the superstitions associated with this artifact. In the meantime, I hope you will

*enjoy having it hanging on your bedroom wall. May it
bring you only good luck!*

Your loving father.

"What is it, Nick?" His mother's voice sounded motherly. Nick had noticed that she had several different ways of speaking. She sounded like Doctor Scientist Price when she spoke to any of her colleagues at work at the Biological Station. She sounded like The Honourable Politician Price when she spoke to the environmental group or media people. And she sounded like Loving Mother Price when she was at home feeling happy and contented.

"It's a medicine stick. It can cast a spell." Nick made his voice sound spooky as he stood in the doorway and shook the thing above his head.

"Don't." Jonathan sounded alarmed. "It's got a scary face."

"Oh, what a lovely souvenir," said Patricia.

Nick felt a tremor spread through the muscles of his arm. Suddenly the stick was so heavy he could scarcely hold it. His arm dropped and the red feathers brushed the floor.

"What's it used for? Did your father say?"

Nick felt very tired. His bones seemed heavy and he was having trouble getting his legs to move. He turned, tossed the stick onto a chair beside his bed and slowly carried the note to his mother in the kitchen. He rested on a bar stool beside the counter as she read it.

"Interesting. The religious practices of different groups of people are fascinating," she said. "Imagine actually believing that grass, a stone and a few feathers can cause supernatural events to occur. Still . . . ." She shrugged. "I suppose it's not so different from modern religion. Except people now understand that symbols are just that. Symbols. They do not, of themselves, have any extraordinary qualities."

I wouldn't be so sure about that, thought Nick, as he stood and dragged himself back into his room. He was too tired to do anything but flop on his bed. He slept for an hour and awoke feeling thick-headed.

The medicine stick was lying on the chair where he had left it. But it was moving! The red feathers pulsed softly like a faintly beating heart. His eyes must be playing tricks on him. He sat on the edge of his bed, opened his eyes very wide, closed them and pressed the palms of his hands against his eyelids. He stayed that way for several seconds, to give his vision a chance to clear.

The feathers were still moving, ever so slightly. It had to be caused by a draft. Or the shadows. He glanced at the tree outside his window. Its branches could sometimes cause objects in his room to appear to shift and waver.

Today the branches were still.

He stood and stepped closer to the stick and stared down at it. The feathers seemed to fold in on themselves, like sea anemones when they are touched.

He scowled. "You can't scare me," he whispered. The face smirked up at him. *Wanna bet?* it seemed to say. He picked it up. It was weightless. There was nothing there. Whoever, or whatever, was living in it had gone to sleep.

Living in it? This is a stone and some feathers, Nick, like Mom said.

Just the same, Nick wished that this were happening some other day. When he was not feeling sort of nervous because of the scarecrow.

Put it out of sight just now. Good idea. Get it out tomorrow. He knelt beside his dresser, opened the bottom drawer, pulled up a pile of folded sweatshirts and laid the stick on the bare wood. Then he gingerly smoothed out the red feathers. Better not wreck the thing. It was, after all, a present from Dad. He let the shirts fall back into place and slammed the drawer shut.

He sat back on his heels.

A gift from his father. Made of straw and a stone and some feathers. One that he "hunted high and low" to find. "May it bring you only good luck," the note said. Just straw

and a stone and some feathers. Sent by his father. Could
he leave it shut up in the bottom of a drawer?

A silver picture hook gleamed on the wall over his
bed. It was waiting. Until the day before it had held a
paint-by-number cocker spaniel that he had done at the
age of nine when he had had chicken pox. Was it just a
day since he had looked at that picture as though seeing it
for the first time? Could it be less than twenty-four hours
since he had taken it down, told his mother that he was
going to buy a map of South America and chucked the
cocker spaniel in a box in the laundry room? Since then
the hook had been waiting. But not for a map. He knew it
as surely as if the hook had spoken. It was waiting for a
parcel from Brazil. Nick did not want a strange medicine
stick hanging over his head while he slept. But he had no
choice. It was too much of a coincidence to be accidental.
A bright silver empty hook — waiting.

He reached into the dresser drawer and felt around.

It was gone!

He pushed both hands under the pile of clothing. Only
soft fleecy fabric rubbed his palms and fingers. He yanked
the drawer open, scooped up clothing in both arms and
threw it on the floor in one tangled bundle.

Clunk! A black sweatshirt hit the floor with a dull thud.

"What's going on in there?" called his mother. "Do I
see clothes flying past the door?"

"Just looking for something. I'll clean up," called Nick,
trying to make his voice sound ordinary.

He carefully unwound the black shirt from the medicine stick and smoothed out its feathers. A half-broken
feather clung to a sleeve, the jagged end embedded in
black threads. Nick, full of remorse, stared at the medicine
stick in his hands. His father had sent him a wonderful
present and he had buried it alive. Then he had tossed it
around like a piece of junk. And broke it.

Buried alive? Come off it, Nick. You're getting anthro-some-

thing. That big word. Anthropomorphic. When you think ani-
mals or things are like people. A scarecrow can't get choked or
stabbed, and a medicine stick can't get buried alive. Because it's
not. Alive.

He pulled the feather from the fabric, leaving a loop of
thread and a small hole. Great! Now he'd wrecked his favourite shirt. He sighed, sat back on his heels again and
tried to figure out a way to repair the quill of the broken
feather. Put a cast on it with a toothpick and Scotch tape?

Better cut it off. He went to the bathroom, got his
mother's nail scissors and snipped through the bent
feather as close to the straw binding as he could manage,
half expecting to hear it say "ouch."

He dropped it into the wastepaper basket. It looked
small and forlorn, lying there amongst crumpled paper,
balled-up Kleenex tissue and torn envelopes. He quickly
snatched it out and wedged the end into a space at the
corner of a picture frame which hung over his dresser. The
picture showed cowboys sitting around a campfire and the
feather settled its half-broken quill around the corner of
the frame with, it seemed to Nick, a contented sigh.

He hung the stick on its silver hook and vowed to
keep it there forever. Because his dad had sent it.

Chapter 9

The medicine stick was behaving itself just fine the next morning. Doing its job. Hanging there giving his room an exotic touch. The scowling face reminded Nick of Jonathan, pretending to be mad. He lifted it down. It was just a stick, a stone and some feathers, as harmless as Nick's old teddy bear. Maybe Allison would like to see it. She liked that old spoon so much. Probably she liked all kinds of unusual things. He put it on his windowsill beside the open window. He should tell his mother that he was going to meet Allison, but she might wonder why he was taking the stick.

Nick wasn't quite sure how to broach the subject. He cleared his throat.

"I'm going on my bike to that place where they used to cut the millstones. Because it's you know . . . um, it's kind of interesting to see the round holes they left. From cutting them. A long time ago. And, and . . . for people who haven't ever been there . . . you know? Going to show them to that girl. Her father is a, a . . . the logging company?" Nick finished quickly and glanced at his mother.

She often did her office work at home, especially during the summer months, and she was working at the kitchen table now on some kind of graph, with temperatures and stuff on it. There were papers with columns of figures and dates strewn around. She wore flat huaraches on her bare feet and a sleeveless pale green blouse tucked into white cotton pants.

"Oh. That's nice. I'm sure she must be feeling the tension. Pretty stressful when things get to this state. I wonder who strung that wire? And the bulldozer business is just — " she shook her head "— absolutely unforgivable. Absolutely.

It's all very mysterious and frightening. Nobody seems to have an inkling of who or why."

Whew! That had been easy. But he might have known what his mother would say. He backed out the door, waved and said, "'Bye then, see you later." Then he scurried around to his bedroom window, grabbed the stick and headed off to meet Allison.

"My mother said it was terrible, the things that happened about the bulldozer and the wire and stuff," said Nick as they pedalled along side by side.

"Oh, that's good. 'Cause I sure think it's terrible, too." Allison flipped her hair away from the back of her neck with one hand.

"And she said she didn't know who could do such a thing," Nick added. "So I don't think it could be any of her friends."

The medicine stick, riding in Nick's carrier, seemed to be bouncing along in a carefree way, enjoying the ride.

They walked their bicycles along a forested path to a sandstone outcropping, where the millstones had been cut. The clearing was about the size of a baseball diamond. Stunted grasses, wildflowers and lichen grew in uneven patches here and there on the shallow little valleys and knolls. More than fifty years earlier two dozen perfectly round holes, each three feet across, had been cut out of the sandstone to make millstones. Now these holes were little ponds.

"They're neat, and so is this," said Allison, as Nick handed her the medicine stick and led the way to the highest knoll where they could sit and look down into the ponds. She brushed the palm of her hand along the red feather plumes and traced the outline of the face with her finger. Her hands were square and solid with the fingernails cut short, just the way Nick thought a girl's hands should be. She smelled nice, too. Not perfume — more like a clean soap smell.

"I thought you'd like to see it. Because it might be old, you know, like the spoon," said Nick.

"What's it for?"

"Oh, here. I brought my dad's letter." Nick pulled it out of his shirt pocket. He *was* getting more like his father every day, putting important things in the same pocket where his dad carried lists.

She read some of the phrases aloud. ". . . identify a criminal . . . cast a spell . . . death unless more powerful magic . . . bring you only good luck. It sounds like the real thing. It really is a neat present, Nick." She turned the stick over. "Look. It's not an ugly face, it's a friendly one."

There was a smiling almond-eyed face on the other side of the stone figure. Why hadn't he noticed it before?

"Where's the book? The one you found?"

Nick jumped up from the warm sandstone where they were sitting and pulled the grubby copy of *Terror on the Island* from his bicycle bag.

"This guy. This Thomas Turner lives here, right?" She laid the medicine stick carefully on the flat stone and arranged the feathers before reaching for the book.

"Uh-huh. Just across the road from us and up a bit."

Allison opened the book and smoothed the title page with her hand. A small soft whitish-grey feather floated up, then settled on a dandelion. "Huh. Somebody must have been reading it in a chicken coop," she said. "So this book could be a clue, then. You found it at the scene of the crime." Allison turned the pages slowly.

Nick frowned. "Could be. Or maybe not. Who knows how it got there? Seems like a funny coincidence, though. It was run over by the bulldozer. Mashed right into the ground."

"So, my dear Watson," said Allison, "we have two crimes: wire strung around trees, and a bulldozer sent crashing down a cliff."

Should I tell her about the scarecrow? Not quite in the same league, but still . . . .

He did tell her.

"Somebody could get killed if this stuff keeps happening." Allison laid the book down, bent her knees and hugged them with both arms.

"Yeah." Nick felt a needle of fear. Somebody *could* get killed.

"Umm." Allison was thinking. "Umm, the guy we saw run away . . . Max, you said?"

Nick nodded.

Allison picked up the feathered stick in her right hand and pulled its length gently through her left one as she spoke. It sure didn't look as though it could ever be evil when she was holding it. It looked like a tropical flower — a frangipani? Nick wasn't sure what a frangipani looked like, but it had a nice name.

"Well, we'll start there," said Allison in a matter-of-fact tone. "I wonder if he reads murder mysteries? Anyway, let's put a . . . you know. A thing on him. What do they call it? On the detective programs. When you watch somebody. A shadow? A spy? A follower?"

Nick laughed. "A tail." He stood up. "But he works shifts, so we'll have to find out when he's at work and when he's at home."

"Right. Let's find out when he's working on the ferry and put a tail on him. Or two tails. Or maybe I should be the head and you can be the tail." She laughed up into his face and danced away across the brown grass.

Nick showed her the frogs and the orange-bellied newts that lived in the perfectly round ponds. He reached for her hand as she walked on the narrow bridges of stone between the holes. They weren't very deep, only about three or four feet. Green algae floated on them like miniature water lilies among the rushes.

"How did they get here? Why are they so absolutely round?" she asked.

"Look." Nick pointed to two three-foot-wide circular

stones with holes in the middle, like doughnuts, lying broken and discarded at the side of the clearing. "They cut them out of the rock. More than fifty years ago. Shipped them all over the world. Millstones — mostly for pulp mills."

"But how did they cut them off at the bottom?"

Nick laughed. "That's what everybody wonders. I think they used small charges of dynamite. Tamped down at the sides."

"It's a perfect place for a picnic," said Allison. "Oh, look at these neat little yellow flowers. Like faces." She bent closer to a small orchid-like blossom growing in a stream that trickled down the rock just at the edge of the tree line. "Why don't more people come here?" she asked. "Why don't they make it into a real park? I bet in the States they would. And they'd call it the only one of its kind in the world, and people would go there by the thousands and . . . . "

"I guess that's why. Because of people by the thousands. Candy wrappers. Film boxes. Initials carved on the sides of the ponds."

She smiled and nodded. "I see what you mean." She picked up the book. "Who's taking charge of the clues?"

"You. You're probably a lot better at keeping track of stuff like that."

"Speaking of keeping track, I haven't been keeping track of the time." Allison reached for Nick's wrist and turned it over to look at his watch. "Oh, I better go. I promised I'd stay with my sisters while my mother goes to town. She's got an appointment or something. Has to get the 4:15 ferry."

They rode their bicycles back without stopping.

Chapter 10

The medicine stick seemed to be fitting in just fine. It sat perfectly still on its hook, smiling face exposed, like a peaceful Buddha. After awhile Nick didn't even bother to check it out every time he went into his room. It had become just one of the furnishings.

Until two days later.

His mother and Jonathan had gone to a staff picnic on Newcastle Island. All the Biological Station employees and their families were invited, and she had said it might be fun for Nick, too. They wouldn't stay late and there would be music and snacks for the teens in the pavilion, and they could probably dance, et cetera. The idea of dancing in front of those teenagers, who probably all thought they were super wonderful because their fathers or mothers were scientists, sent cold shivers up and down Nick's spine.

He decided to stay home and go for one of Dad's special walks. He hadn't done that since his father had left, so maybe it was about time he did it — just to think about his dad and practise to see if he could make it as interesting as those walks had been. And *maybe* invite Allison to go sometime.

At first the walk seemed very sad. He kept hearing and seeing and smelling things that reminded him of Dad. Butterflies, fungi, huckleberries, pine cones, fireweed, grasshoppers, birds. But gradually the empty feeling got filled up with the quiet of the woods. He decided he would ask Allison if she would like to go. Next Sunday. He could probably teach her a lot about insects and stuff like that. But what if she thought it was boring? Boring? Allison? He couldn't imagine Allison looking bored.

He headed home. He would put on his bathing trunks, get a cold drink and one of Jonathan's *Mad* magazines and take them down to the little beach in front of the house.

He stepped into the kitchen and stopped.

He held his breath and listened. Nothing but the hum of the refrigerator and a fly buzzing at the kitchen window. He strained to hear. There it was again. A soft thud. He shivered and sniffed the air. Something seemed strange. As though somebody or something had been there.

"Anybody home?" he called.

Thud.

He moved quietly through the house in the direction of the noise. It seemed to be coming from his mother's bedroom.

Just the door! He breathed a sigh of relief. The door leading from the room onto the little outside patio was slightly ajar. Funny she'd leave it like that. She didn't often open that door. He closed and latched it.

Nick walked back into the living room. There it was again. That feeling that somebody was watching him. He turned his head slowly, looking from one corner of the room to the next. His eyes lingered on each piece of furniture.

He gasped. His heart stopped beating. His knees started to dissolve. The photograph. His mother's face in the family photograph had been scratched out. Not just scratched — gouged out. With red ink. Fear rose in his throat and his hands shook. He scarcely breathed as he crept through his mother's and Jonathan's bedrooms, opening closets, looking under beds.

He headed for his own room and stopped dead in his tracks as a bright flash of light spun around the living room. He ran to the patio doors and stared out. Of course! Just a cabin cruiser, moored in the bay, bobbing around on the waves, its windshield sending reflected sunlight in random patterns.

Geez, Nick, where's your cool? You've seen flashes like that dozens of times.

He turned away, and the room looked fuzzy and dark compared to the bright sparkle of the sea.

I have to be calm, like Dad.

Nick shook himself, rubbed his eyes and concentrated on being calm as he hurried to his room. Everything was as usual, except . . . the medicine stick was gone! And there was blood! On the carpet. Oozing out from under his bed. He yanked back the chenille spread. The ugly gaping face snarled at him.

It laughed out loud.

Nick shuddered, jumped back and stared. It laughed again. The sound reminded him of something. Birds. Ibises? No. A crow. Imitating eagles and seagulls. Perched on a branch just outside his open window. Nick felt a small surge of relief in the pit of his stomach. Just a crow outside the window and red feathers on the carpet, not blood.

But how did the medicine stick get down there? Surely it couldn't have fallen by itself. He jumped up on his bed and examined the silver hook. It was bent. Did somebody yank it down? Who? Why? He felt, suddenly, as though he couldn't get enough air, and his skin was itchy. He went outside.

The scarecrow looked like itself. A kingfisher screeched as it dove from a tree branch into the water below. It came back with a small fish in its beak. The otters had been up the bank again — the pungent smell of seashell and animal dung mixture was like no other. The crow squawked, the gulls cried and there was the sound of a distant chainsaw. Loggers? No, too close. Somebody cutting up a beach log for firewood.

The world was at peace, and gradually Nick's hands stopped shaking. His heartbeat slowed down a little.

I did most of it to myself. Imagination in overdrive. I've got to get myself together. Think like a computer.

Computer thoughts helped a little. Nick fed the information in and discovered that there was really only one item that wouldn't compute. The medicine stick getting off its hook and onto the floor was a little worrisome, but things like that *can* happen. He remembered a hall mirror getting smashed and waking them all in the middle of the night, because its hook suddenly let go. But the scribbled-out face of his mother in the picture was impossible to rationalize. He tried it from every angle. Kids playing jokes? Loggers trying to scare her? Somebody she worked with jealous of her recent promotion? Jonathan, mad about something? Maybe she would know of some reason . . . .

"That's sick," she said, when she saw it. She held the photograph and shook her head. "I guess we'll have to start locking doors. What a nuisance. Somebody has come into this house to do deliberate vandalism. I'm furious. And tired."

She shoved the picture into the top drawer of the sideboard and rubbed the back of her hand across her forehead. "Would you get Jonathan a peanut butter sandwich, Nick? I think I'll lie down."

"Sure. Are you okay?"

"Yes. Just tired." She walked into her bedroom with slow steps.

Chapter 11

Nick's mother was under the weather all the next day, but by evening she seemed fine again. Nick offered to get the supper ready, so she could relax outside. He was glad when she poured herself a little glass of sherry and carried it out to the deck. That meant she really was feeling better.

"Sure you can manage, Nick? Where's Jonnie, he should be helping." She set the sherry on a small round patio table, kicked off her slippers, settled herself on the lounge and stretched her legs.

"No. It's fine, Mom. I'll just do baked potatoes and some fish. That should be okay for your stomach, don't you think? Easy to digest?"

"Yes, Nick." She smiled at him. "You really are one of the good guys, you know."

"Jonathan is over at Michael's. Mrs. Pickering said she'd make sure he got home okay," said Nick.

"Good. Thanks."

I hope she's okay tomorrow because Allison and I are going to put a tail on Max.

But the next morning she had a relapse. She dragged herself around the kitchen, cooking Cream of Wheat, but she looked pale and tired. "You said you were going to town today, Nick?" she asked.

He nodded. "Will you be all right, Mom?"

"Long as Jonathan is — " she stopped moving, put her hand on the countertop and leaned against it "— looked after."

"Sure, Mom."

Should I leave her alone with the medicine stick?

"Maybe he can go to the Pickerings' again. I'll phone." She moved to the telephone and dropped heavily onto the swivel chair beside it.

Get real, Nick. How could the medicine stick hurt her?

Jonathan had his Lego castle, complete with knights, a princess, a drawbridge and sailing ships, spread out all over the kitchen table. He looked up at the sound of his name. "Sure. I can go to Michael's place. That will be A-okay with me," he said.

"Put that Lego away first," said his mother as she dialled.

It was A-okay with everybody, and Nick left his mother settled in bed and headed off to meet Allison.

The ferry terminal property in Descanso Bay had two small buildings and a parking lot for about forty cars. One building housed the Ladies and Gents bathrooms, and the smallest one, a waiting room located right at the top of the ramp, could shelter two dozen people in a pinch. The ferry provided hourly service between Gabriola Island and Nanaimo. It held sixty-two cars and had four passenger lounges, two on each side of the car deck.

"We shouldn't get on together," said Allison, as they parked their bikes beside the waiting room. "You go to the right side, I'll go to the left, and we'll both keep our eyes open."

"Are we going to get off on the other side?"

"What do you think? Maybe one of us should wait and come back on the next ferry. Or . . . ."

Nick's heart sagged with disappointment. Tailing a suspect was fun as long as Allison was there — he'd be able to catch glimpses of her as she moved around her side of the boat. But to come back on different trips didn't sound at all appealing.

"There he is," whispered Nick. "He's just starting the afternoon shift."

Max ducked under the barrier and walked down the ramp to wait with the other crew members. His lunch pail looked heavy and twice as big as anyone else's. He kicked at a bolt on the side of the piling as he waited.

"I think we should stick together," said Nick.

"Yeah, let's," said Allison. "As long as he doesn't know."

A roar of skateboards on pavement. Two boys hurtled down the hill, their bodies swooping and bending, hair whipping back in the wind, eyes half-closed with concentration. They circled Nick and Allison with ollies and slides, then jumped off the boards and flipped them into their hands. Allison moved aside.

"Yo, Price. What you been doing? Haven't seen you for a week. You didn't go to the car races yesterday. Thought you'da been there. Phoned this morning. Where's your board?"

Beaver and Grolinski and Nick were the only fourteen-year-old boys on the island, so they hung around together. Actually, Grolinski was fifteen but he had failed a grade — they didn't call it failing anymore, they called it Self-Determined Progress. But it didn't fool anybody.

Grolinski was big. Not taller than Nick, but more muscular. If he had missed keeping up with the kids his age in school, he made up for it elsewhere. It was Grolinski who usually decided what they should do. Especially the somewhat illegal or more daring things. Like smoking in the passenger lounge. Except now smoking wasn't allowed in any of the lounges, and Nick was glad. Smoking and doing stuff like that wasn't all that exciting in his books. Still, he didn't have any other choice of friends here.

"Go home and get your board. Come over on the next ferry. We'll hang around in the mall," Grolinski said to Nick.

"Ah, no. Can't today. Got a dentist appointment." What if Beaver and Grolinski found out about Allison? They'd hang around. Give him a bad time.

"Thought you went a few weeks ago. You said you didn't have any cavities," said Beaver. Beaver's own teeth always looked well scrubbed and no longer seemed too big for his face, as they had when he started school and picked up his nickname.

"Yeah. Well, I didn't, but then I had a toothache, and he found something that needs fixing," said Nick. "Just a very small hole, but you know . . . ."

Just then Max opened the gate at the top of the ramp, and Nick glanced back, hoping to send a smile in Allison's direction. A gesture that would say, I've got to humour these guys right now, but we're still together. Allison was looking the other way. "I don't think I'll go in there," he nodded toward the lounge.

"C'mon, c'mon, c'mon," said Grolinski. "Don't be a pain in the butt." He lowered his voice. "Got a plug."

Chewing tobacco? Yuck. Nick thought fast. "Better not. Going to the dentist."

"What's the dentist got to do with it, Dork? You can rinse it out." Grolinski's look seemed to say that passing up chewing tobacco for the sake of the dentist was in the same category as avoiding the video arcade in favour of the library.

"My breath. He'll smell it on my breath."

"Shit! What's the big deal? Just come and rap, then." Grolinski put his bent elbow on Nick's shoulder and leaned down hard.

Nick stepped back. "Hey guys. I want to stay outside. Okay?" His voice rose in irritation. "Do I have to ask permission? Okay if I stay outside? Just 'cause I feel like it? Okay?"

There was the faint possibility that the other two would stay outside with him, but Nick was pretty sure they would prefer the lounge, where their tobacco-chewing behaviour was more daring — much greater odds of being seen by someone who might tell their parents.

"Let's go. Let him stay outside if he wants." Beaver walked toward the lounge door. Good old Beaver. Always the peacemaker.

The ferry was crowded. It was always crowded in August. Tourists and summer residents swarmed to and from the island like schools of herring going in opposite directions. The throb of the engines grew loud. Nick smelled diesel fuel and felt an extra blast of heat on his already hot face as he walked the narrow space between cars and passenger lounges past the open engine-room door.

The front section of the boat looked like a cruise advertisement. People leaned against the metal sides and pointed fingers and cameras, or held up children, argued, ate candy or stared into the distance dreamy-eyed. Islands floated by, lifting sandstone cliffs and tree-topped hills into the sunshine. Eagles soared overhead.

Nick sauntered casually over to Allison and spoke to her out of the corner of his mouth. "I have to get off. Told those guys I'm going to the dentist."

"Okay. Meet you in the mall." What a sensible girl.

Allison was a perfect spy. She looked as though her only interest in life was looking good. She moved back and forth among the cars, flipping her hair with the back of her hand, pausing to gaze out to sea with a faraway look, smiling sweetly at two small girls who were chasing each other around and "accidentally" bumping into Max. She should be an actress, thought Nick.

Max crossed to Nick's side of the ferry and climbed the narrow stairs to the bridge. Why was he carrying his lunch pail? The crew's lounge was near the engine room. Max set the pail on a steel girder, looked down and moved back out of sight.

Nick wedged himself in between a life raft and the railing and lifted his face to the sun, looking, he hoped, like he was just catching a few rays. He could see Max, but Max could also see him. He scowled at Nick's upturned face. Nick twisted around and studied the steam belching from the pulp mill in the distance.

He turned back just in time to get the impression that

something had left Max's hand and plunged down into the
water. He strained his eyes in the direction of the splash.
There seemed to be rippling circles and some bubbles, but
it was hard to tell on the already bubbling sea.

The trip took eighteen minutes when the weather was
calm, as it was today. The engine noise lessened and the
ship slowed. People zipped up camera cases, called to children, folded maps and moved toward cars and trucks and
campers and motor homes. Young people claimed bicycles
and backpacks. The lounge doors opened and mothers carrying babies, old people carrying canes, people of all ages
carrying overnight bags and briefcases, and Beaver and
Grolinski carrying skateboards walked spread-legged on
the swaying deck. Together they waited for the ferry crew
to punch the right buttons, move the right levers, throw
the ropes over the right hooks, undo the chain and nod to
the foot passengers to go.

Nick and Allison climbed the ramp and crossed the
street to the shopping mall.

"I'm pretty sure he threw something in the water,"
said Nick, as they walked along the centre aisle. The smell
of chocolate and ice cream made him feel hungry. "You
want a Coke, or something?" he asked. This was the first
time they had been "out together" in public, and he was
feeling shy and awkward again.

"Sure," said Allison. "As long as it's dutch."

*Guess I did it right. She said sure. Maybe I'm not so bad
with girls after all.*

Nick happily led Allison through the shortcut corridor
to the cafeteria. They took their drinks to the farthest corner.

"Those guys. Are they friends of yours?" Allison stirred
her drink with a straw and the ice clinked against the glass.

"Yeah. School friends."

"Not summer holiday friends?"

"Well, yeah." Nick shrugged. "Sort of. But all they want
to do is go skateboarding. Morning, noon and night. I like

skateboarding as much as the next guy, but morning, noon and night?" Nick felt a prick of guilt. He had gone skateboarding just as often as the others, until . . . .

"What's the matter? You look worried. Has something else happened?"

"Well, no. Yes. A picture. Of our family. When I got home on Saturday, the picture had, had . . . . My mother's face was scribbled out."

"What?" Allison looked shocked.

"Yeah. With a red pen."

"That's, that's horrible! Who would do that?"

Nick shrugged. "And, she seems, I don't know. She seems to be so tired, and, you know, different. Almost . . . almost . . . like one of those spells Dad told about."

"Like a magic spell?" Allison said the word "magic" like it was something alive.

Nick nodded and stared at the plastic tablecloth.

"It's not magic, Nick." She leaned forward and put her hand on his. It felt warm and soft and made the back of his hand tingle. "There's no such thing as voodoo spells. Not here. Maybe in Brazil, but that's because people believe in them. They get sick, or better, or, or — " she shuddered " — die, because they think they will. That's all."

"Yeah. You're right," said Nick. His mother probably just had the flu, like she said. But there were still some real things to worry about. A scribbled-out face in a photograph and a strangled and stabbed scarecrow. Not to mention wire and bulldozer accidents. Accidents that happened accidentally on purpose.

"Nicholas!" Allison put her elbows on the table and leaned toward him. "If they can do it, you know. Make things happen because they believe they can? Then so can we. We can undo the — " she made her voice husky " — voodoo spell. Let's make a pact. Let's always, always act as if we can handle it, whatever 'it' is."

Nick felt relieved. He could smell the clean soap smell

again and her blue eyes were wide. Her lips were pressed firmly together and her hands were clasped in a pleading way.

"Sure! Good idea," said Nick. If Allison had suggested at that moment that they take the next plane to the Amazon jungle to consult with a real witch doctor, he would have said, "Sure! Good idea."

"Who are the suspects so far? We've got Max, who was definitely at the scene of the crime. Something we heard in the bushes, could have been somebody else at the scene of the crime, but that's an unknown. So we have an unknown suspect. And Thomas Turner's book was there. Does that make him a suspect?" Allison was holding up two fingers.

"I don't think so. He's always hanging around things like that. Accidents and stuff. Looking for ideas. And why would he be carrying a copy of his own book?"

"Too bad your dad didn't tell you how to make that stick work. To make a criminal confess, or whatever it was."

"Oh, he did." Nick smacked his forehead with the palm of his hand. "I forgot to tell you. I got another letter. Tells all about this, this . . . worship thing. It's a ritual. He saw them doing it."

Allison sat up straight and smiled. "Then we'll do it. Does it have to be at night, or what?"

"It's supposed to be in a secret place. Like a special hut, or something."

"We'll find a secret place and we'll do our own voodoo." Allison looked as matter-of-fact as though she had just announced that it was time to wash the dishes. "And we have to believe we can solve this case. Nick and Allison solve the mystery of the . . . ." She paused.

"Bulldozer, scarecrow, wrecked picture, broken wrist," said Nick, smiling. "Pretty long title for a made-for-TV movie."

"Yeah." Allison giggled. "Okay, then. We'll just have

to use our names. Price . . . McKeghnie . . . McPrice? No, I know. How about 'The Very First Case of the Timex Two'?"

"Why Timex?"

"You know that old ad? 'It takes a licking and keeps on ticking?' That's us. We can take a licking, and . . . . "

"Yeah," said Nick. "Perfect," said Nick. "We can," said Nick. His heart bumped around as Allison reached over to shake hands on the newly christened partnership.

Chapter 12

Nick had a lot of trouble feeling like he could keep on ticking when he got home. He tried not to think of the new horrible thing he had found, and then he tried to think of it in the way Allison would, in a practical, problem-solving way.

The blouse, his mother's good blouse, was hanging on the clothesline in shreds.

And she had been home all the time. How did he — if it was a he — do it? It had been cut with something sharp, not ripped. It flapped in the breeze in a tangle of long white ribbons.

Nick was even more worried when he saw his mother, still weak and tired, still lying in bed. He wasn't sure what day of the week it was by the time he carried a cup of chicken broth and a glass of skim milk into her bedroom. She hadn't eaten all day.

She was wearing her housecoat and her skin looked like dough. Her forehead was speckled with perspiration. Her hair, usually shining and thick, was damp and stringy, the curls clinging to the sides of her face like they were pasted there.

"It's just the flu, Nick," she said. "Don't worry. Some crackpot . . . ." She plucked at the bedcover with thumb and forefinger.

"Pardon?"

"Sorry. What was it?" She turned her attention back to Nick.

"About some crackpot something."

What's the matter with her?

"Some crackpot . . . phone call . . . photograph . . . ." She closed her eyes and frowned. "Some crackpot . . . not going to. Not going to . . . frighten me."

"What phone call? What?" Nick swallowed.

His mother looked exactly like someone who was under a spell. Her eyes were glazed and her hand shook as she tried to pick up the glass of milk.

"Let me call the doctor, Mom."

"Nick, it's the flu. If I don't feel better, after . . . in the morning . . . call him . . . okay?"

"Okay." He swallowed hard and tried to clear his throat. There seemed to be something stuck in it. Fear?

Nick didn't feel as though he could handle one more unpleasant surprise, until he walked into his bedroom and found that there was another one to handle whether he liked it or not. The medicine stick was acting weird. It seemed to have a smirk on its face, like it knew some nasty secret. Nick stood in front of it, trying to outstare it, but the face leered back. Its gaping mouth was forming the word "evil."

I gotta get it out of here. *Sorry, chum.* He reached for it. *You gotta go.* But it didn't want to come off the hook. *Geez, it either falls off by itself, or it won't come off at all.*

Come to think of it, though, he had bent the hook extra tight when he hung it back up that day. The day he had been so paranoid, thinking the whole world was out to get him. Or his mother.

The medicine stick felt heavy, and it made his hand tingle as he carried it out to the woodshed.

Imagination working overtime, again.

He hid it behind a pile of kindling. Anything, *anything,* that might help his mother get better was worth a try.

Even if you are a present from Dad. Just can't take a chance. Sorry.

The telephone was ringing.

Or was it part of the dream?

Petroglyphs with blue eyes were following him along a jungle path. He could see a telephone booth in the distance with bright red, blue and yellow birds painted on its sides. He started to run. He must answer the telephone. He could hear the petroglyphs crashing along the path behind him. Their eyes were flashing beams of bright light. Five howling monkeys were squabbling about which one would open the door of the booth.

Nick sat bolt upright in bed. The telephone really was ringing. In the middle of the night? He lunged into the kitchen and grabbed it. He glanced at the clock. 3:35.

"Hello? Hello?"

Must be Brazil. He held his breath.

Maybe it's Dad. Or maybe something has happened to Dad.

A sharp pain caught in his throat. Muffled noises reminded him of something. Faint drumbeats and a high-pitched sobbing whistle. And a bird. A parakeet, or ibis? *What kind of a sound does an ibis make?*

A voice. Faint, muffled and husky. "Tell her to go."

"Who? Who?" Nick's own voice echoed through the receiver.

"Tell her to leave the island." The words sounded gasping and urgent.

"Who? Where? Go where?"

Click. There was a wall of silence.

Nick's hand went limp as he dropped the telephone back in its cradle.

Mom! Is Mom okay? She said something about a phone call. Maybe it was the same kind.

He ran through the living room and tiptoed down the hall toward her room.

"Nick? Is that you? Did I hear the phone?" Her sleep-filled voice came through the partly opened door. At least she sounded normal, now.

"Yeah. It's okay. Wrong number."

"Oh. What time is it?"

"Twenty to four."

"Thanks."

Nick heard the swish of riffling bedcovers and his mother's yawn.

Jonathan! Is Jonathan okay?

Nick stood silently, one hand on the doorknob, and leaned toward Jonathan's bed. Curly hair moved against a white pillow. He heard a small deep sigh. Nick closed the door just as the telephone screamed again.

He stopped breathing as he picked up the receiver.

"Is Patricia Price there? It's urgent." The deep voice sounded familiar, not at all like the previous caller.

"Um, she's not feeling . . . ." But his mother was beside him, holding out her hand.

"What do you want?" she snapped into the mouth-piece. She listened for several seconds. "Oh, sure. I'm on my way. No. I'll take my car." She slammed down the telephone and raced back to her bedroom, calling to Nick as she ran. "Fire. At the community hall."

"But, Mom. You can't go. You're sick." Nick followed her.

"I'm fine now. Just fine." She was pulling on clothing over her nightgown. "Really, Nick. I couldn't be feeling better." She put both palms briefly against his cheeks.

"Have you seen the car keys?" She looked puzzled as she stood by the kitchen door looking at the row of hooks where various keys were hung.

"No." Nick stood beside her and looked.

"Oh, I know. They're in my jacket pocket. Will you get them? In the hall closet?"

She was tying her shoelace as he handed her the keys. "I'll phone the minute I get a chance." She was out the door. Patricia Price was a fire department volunteer — one of the auxiliary members whose job it was to go and rouse extra firefighters while telephones and beeping pagers were used to call the regular crew. Auxiliaries were used only when the woods were dry and the fire hazard was extremely high.

Nick felt a twinge of relief. She was feeling better. He locked the door and turned off the kitchen light.

He didn't like to think that somebody out there in a boat, or lurking in the bushes along the driveway, could look in and see him in the brightly lit kitchen. Somebody who dialled the Prices' telephone number and made weird sounds. Somebody who sent messages by stabbing a scarecrow and wrecking a picture. And ripping a blouse. Somebody who sent a bulldozer crashing over a cliff.

Somebody who set fire to the community hall?

His heart lurched. What if there wasn't really a fire? What if somebody just wanted to lure his mother away for . . . ? He ran into his bedroom and looked out. A cloud of smoke reflected a glow of red on the horizon. Just about where the community hall would be.

He moved into the living room. The moon made a silver path on the water in the bay. He looked into Jonathan's room.

"Nick? Did Mom go somewhere?" asked a sleepy voice.

"Yeah. There's a fire, but it's okay. I'm here." He lay on the bed with his arm around his brother and listened for strange noises.

Chapter 13

Nick hoped Allison would be there when they went to see the charred remains of the community hall after breakfast that morning, but of course she wasn't. Her parents were probably worried about being the outsiders when all these nasty things were happening. Afraid that the loggers would be blamed for doing it — in retaliation for the bulldozer "accident."

A few chairs lay blistered and twisted in the smoking ruins. A metal frame and some thin wires were in a heap of rubble where the piano had stood. Some wire coat hangers, a tin cup and a bronze bell were still recognizable. The fire chief and the two island RCMP constables were talking quietly. One of the policemen was making notes. Both the North End and the South End fire trucks were parked on the grass nearby. Firemen were patrolling the ruins, raking through the debris.

Angry voices mingled as the Prices got out of the car.

"Man, that fire was set."

"Those crazy loggers . . . . "

"I don't know where they're coming from."

"Like, this is bad news, right? This is going too far, am I right?"

Aurora Skye, who was nine, looked as though she were at a birthday party. "I saw the fire," she said to Jonathan. "I saw it with my very own eyes. The flames going up high. Higher than a mountain. All red and orange and blue. Like, like, humungous."

Soon a small crowd had gathered. They reminded each other that the hall was only two years old and talked about the hours of hard labour and the community-raised money that had gone into its construction.

"If it was deliberately set, the investigators will find that out," said Patricia calmly. "And they'll probably find out who did it, too. In the meantime we can help each other deal with our anger and frustration in a way that is not destructive. I certainly feel very hurt and angry at the possibility that it was deliberate, but even if that is so, it may have had nothing at all to do with logging."

She is pretty good at that kind of stuff, thought Nick. And people listen when she talks.

"Oh, sure," said a tall man wearing suspenders that seemed to hitch his pants up too high. His legs looked very long and the rest of his body looked short. "Just a great big coincidence. A bulldozer is shoved off a cliff. The loggers blame us. Our hall is burned down . . . . Sure. It was an act of God." Nick had seen him before. He had an old converted fishboat at the Silva Bay docks, painted with rainbows and balloons and a sign that said *Uncle Ike's Magic Lantern Show. Six Bits a Head.*

Nick hadn't been sure what six bits meant at first, but it was Jonathan who had asked. Two-bits is a quarter, six-bits is seventy-five cents. How many six-bits did the magic lantern show man donate, to feel so strongly that the hall was partly his?

A newspaper reporter from *The Daily Free Press* arrived with a notebook and a camera, and began to interview the bystanders. Aurora tugged at the man's sleeve, trying to tell him about the flames that were humungous.

Nick wandered past the smoking ruins and walked among the salal and alders in the field behind the hall. The air was sweet and clean after the acrid smoke, and he breathed deeply. He felt tired and confused. Too many happenings. Too many out-of-control frightening things.

He thought about his father in the Amazon forest and wondered if he ever felt helpless and afraid. If he did, he would do something about it, not moon around feeling sorry for himself.

It all started when the loggers came.

The loggers. Think! Think! Think! The bulldozer accident could have been caused by island people, although Nick couldn't think of anybody he knew who would do that. Just the same, when people get really mad, strange things happen. And the fire might have been set just to get even for the bulldozer.

Allison. I've got to talk to her. She's right. We'll solve it. The Timex Two.

He sighed and imagined all the mysteries solved and differences settled — like lawyers and judges are supposed to do it, and, and . . . the Prime Minister phoned — he wanted to give them medals. The crowds cheered, and he held Allison's hand and raised it, acknowledging the applause. His mother's eyes were filled with tears.

Isn't that a cricket chirping? Do they have crickets at 24 Sussex Drive? He was back among the alders and salal.

He sat down under a tree with his chin in his hands and thought. They had to solve the mystery. Solve the mystery. But what if the mystery couldn't be solved? All mysteries *could* be solved, it just took common sense.

But what about UFOs and ESP and spooky stuff like that? AND MEDICINE STICKS! *What if . . . naw, but just what if . . . .*

Maybe the magic of the stick really was powerful. Achuara Indians thought so. And not only them. Lots of people believed in witchcraft and black magic.

What if nobody can stop it?

Did it make his mother sick? Should he throw it in the ocean? Get rid of it altogether? Nonsense! Nothing would get solved if people just gave up and didn't try. It would be easy to say it was magic and that's that. He hugged his knees and looked up into space as he concentrated.

Look for clues. That's what detectives in novels do. They watch everything and everybody very carefully — notice things that nobody else sees.

He looked around.

And then he saw something. Something on a wild rose bush with rose hips starting to turn red. Something on a branch near the top. Something silk and silvery, glistening in the sunlight. He jumped up and carefully removed a scrap of fabric from the thorns. It was charred around the edges and smelled of burnt material and something else. The label was folded in two; one side was so badly burned and stained that although there seemed to be the faint imprint of some words on it, he could not decipher anything that made sense. He turned it over. It was made of metallic silver fabric, and embroidered on it in black was some printing ... *en Needle Club,* followed by a series of names. The names did not mean a thing to him. Why names? And why so many? Surely the trademark of the manufacturer could not include all those names?

And why did it smell like that? Sort of like ... gasoline. That was it. Maybe the garment, whatever it was, was soaked in gasoline to help start the fire. And maybe the label was loose, anyway. Nick had often seen labels like that, hanging by a thread or two. So when it started to burn it was caught by a draft and blown onto the rose bush.

This was serious business. Better show the police, for sure. But maybe he should show it to Allison first? Since they were a team. Anyway, you couldn't find fingerprints on fabric, so there shouldn't be that much hurry.

He looked around. Through the trees he could see people milling around, but nobody seemed to be looking his way. He slipped the label into his shirt pocket.

Chapter 14

Nick had made up his mind he was not going to feel helpless and afraid. Well, actually he hoped he could *stop* feeling helpless and afraid. And he could . . . except when he thought about his mother. The scarecrow and the picture and the blouse could all be kids' pranks, nothing to do with anything else. The phone call might have been a wrong number. And the so-called flu was probably really the flu. But she seemed to get over it awfully fast.

His determination to stop feeling helpless lasted for forty-five minutes. Until they got home and he went to the woodshed for a rake. His mother had decided to rake leaves. "Very therapeutic," she said, "raking leaves."

His mother's bedroom window was only twelve feet from the woodshed doorway, but it wasn't until he had disentangled the rake from among the other long-handled tools and turned to leave the shed that Nick noticed the words.

LEAVE OR DIE. It was written with white foam of some kind. On the outside of the window. But it might as well have been spelled out in black paint in letters six feet high. It was so, so ugly.

Nick dropped the rake, turned back into the shed and snatched the medicine stick down from where he had hidden it behind a bundle of kindling on top of a pile of stacked wood. It was smirking again. It seemed to be saying *Ha! Thought you could get rid of me, did you?* He flung it on the chopping block beside the axe, muttered, "I'll be back to take care of you," and rushed out.

He clenched his fists, stood on tiptoe, scooped a little of the foam onto his index finger. He sniffed . . . it had a faintly perfumed smell that reminded him of his father.

Shaving cream! The message was written in shaving cream.

"What's your hurry, Nick?" His mother reached for the rake he shoved at her.

"Got to turn on the hose. Plants are dying," he gasped and hurried around the house to spray the window. The hateful message slithered down and dissolved into nothing.

Maybe I shouldn't have done that. Maybe I should have let Mom see it. But Dad wouldn't. Dad would say, "Don't give that sort of thing any recognition at all. Just ignore it, then the people who are responsible can't get any pleasure out of their so-called jokes."

Besides, Dad would protect Mom from stuff like that, much as he could. Problem is, I don't know what, or who, I'm protecting her from.

Nick stumbled back to the shed. Could the medicine stick possibly have anything to do with it? The stick was smiling up at him, its red feathers fluttering down over the edge of the block of cedar they used to chop kindling. Nick picked up the axe and raised it over his head.

Hang on there Nick! Are you sure you really want to do this? Chop up a present from Dad?

Of course not. He had just panicked for a minute or two. It was just the "leave or die" message getting to him. So what should he do? He would take the stick back to its silver hook and refuse to even think about supernatural stuff. But when he lifted the stick, the face seemed to wink in the direction of the woodpile, so he put it back behind the kindling. *Just for now.*

So what next? I won't — will not — believe in magic. Only one thing to do then. Make a list. Whether Mom likes it or not. I'm going to make a list of everything and then decide about telling the police. Get Allison to help me figure out what to do. And I have to show her the label soon as I can.

After a lot of tries, and head-scratching, and crossed-out words, and scrunched-up paper, Nick came up with a list he thought was pretty good.

Monday, August 9th
* *loggers tried to start*
* *scarecrow choked*
* *wire in trees: Mr. McKeghnie broke wrist*
Tuesday, August 10th
* *bulldozer crashed*
* *Max ran away from scene of crime*
Wednesday, August 11th
* *found Thomas Turner's book*
* *dartboard on scarecrow*
* *medicine stick came in mail*
Saturday, August 14th
* *Mom's picture gouged*
Monday, August 16th
* *Mom sick*
* *Mom's blouse ripped*
Tuesday, August 17th
* *phone call "Tell her to leave the island" 3:30 AM*
* *community hall burned*
* *found burned scrap of stuff: "en Needle Club" and some names: "Bill Nash, Judy Maybee, Eta Burr, June Smith, Carol Cleaver, Bernice Lusk, Neil Ford, Brenda Storm." Smells of gasoline*
* *shaving cream message: "Leave or Die"*

He met Allison that afternoon. She thought his list was better than pretty good.

"It puts it all right here, where you can see it. Clear as day. I guess we should give the police that burnt label. It is real evidence, don't you think?" Allison looked at him as though he would know exactly what to do. But he didn't.

"Yeah. We should, I guess."

"Let's just wait," said Allison. "A couple hours can't make that much difference. And we've got to keep on with Max."

So here they were. Keeping on with Max. The two burning questions regarding Max were: did he wear clothes with a label that said *en Needle Club;* and did he use an electric razor, or a straight razor and shaving cream? And . . . did he like to read Thomas Turner mysteries?

It was not easy, sneaking up on Max's house. It was set well back from the road and surrounded by tall trees and waist-high salal, except for a weedy yard where several old cars stood in various stages of dismemberment. Oil pans, mufflers, radiators, car doors, bumpers, carburetors and various other metal and rubber accoutrements lay about. It appeared to be washday. There was laundry hanging on the line.

"Oh-oh. There's a dog," said Nick. The animal popped up from nowhere like a very fierce jack-in-the-box, ears erect. It barked and lurched against the chain that held it to a verandah post. Chickens squawked and ran and flew off the low verandah in bursts of fuss and feathers.

Allison moved closer to Nick. "Maybe we should get out of here," she whispered. "They can hear that racket in Tuktoyuktuk."

"Not yet. Let's just check out his clothes on the line. See what labels are in them. There can't be anybody home. I wish I had a bone. Or knew his name." Nick called softly to the dog, "It's okay, guy. There, there. Nice doggie." He skirted the yard toward the clothesline. Allison followed.

The dog stopped barking and stood with its forelegs apart, the hair on the back of its neck bristling. It bared its teeth and growled far back in its throat. The chickens stopped flapping and complaining, and clucked and pecked around a cherry tree.

Nick and Allison stood under the clothesline and looked up. Sheets, towels, shirts and underwear flapped and billowed in the wind. The fresh breezy smell of clean clothes wafted downward.

"We need something to stand on," said Nick. An old

wooden highchair stood near the back door. He carried it to the clothesline. "You watch for cars," he added. "If anybody comes, we'll run along that path at the back there. Lay low until the coast is clear." He was beginning to sound like a real detective.

The dog gave two short barks and its chain rattled. Allison jumped. Then she held the chair steady. Nick climbed up, caught a flapping shirt collar and looked at it closely. Then he reached for a pair of light-orange-coloured sweatpants.

"What the hell are you two up to?" A loud threatening voice. Max stood at the corner of the house, looking more surprised than angry.

"Umm ... ah ... we're just looking for something," said Nick.

"You're what?" snarled Max. He walked toward them with his hands on his hips. "Get down."

Nick jumped. He lost his balance. He clutched at the orange sweatpants. The verandah post where the line was attached swayed and creaked. The hook pulled out with a grinding screech. A fat white hen ran for its life. The clothesline snapped to the ground. Laundry like oddly shaped parachutes ballooned down with Nick in the middle. He fell to his knees. A large sheet printed with antique cars settled slowly over him.

"Oh, I'm sorry. All your nice clean clothes." Allison gasped and groaned as she pulled the sheet up so Nick could crawl out. He unwound a 1929 Hupmobile from his wrist and the sweatpants from his neck. He stood up.

"You're the Price kid, aren't you?" said Max with a scowl. The dark stubble on his usually clean-shaven face made him look even more grim. "What in the bleeding blazes are you up to? Stealing clothes?"

"No, sir. Sorry, sir." Nick tried to remove clothespins with one hand and gather up laundry with the other while Allison was lifting the wire and unwinding socks and towels.

"Leave the bleeding clothes alone and tell me what

you're doing here," shouted Max. He stepped forward to stand directly in front of Nick.

Nick tried to think of something amusing to say. The situation could certainly use some lightening up. "Guess we should use hot air balloons. For a job like this ... sir," he added.

"Use what?"

"Hot air balloons. You know, come down from above to . . . ." He trailed off as Max shook his head impatiently.

"You listen to me, you little punk. And listen good." He grabbed both of Nick's arms in a strong grip. "Quit trying to get out of this by talking about hot air. You better come up with a good reason for messing around with my clothesline, and come up with it fast. Or I'm going to phone your mother. 'Course, she probably put you up to this." He thrust his face closer to Nick's and looked disgusted. "She's one of them save the forest freaks, isn't she?" He released Nick's arms. "What the hell would anybody in their right mind be doing fooling around with a frigging clothesline? Except to steal clothes."

"Mr. Max," said Allison, with a tentative smile. "We got a job, you see. With a soap company. The Clean and Bright soap company. We find out how clean people's laundry is ... you know ... and then find out what kind of soap they use ... and . . . ." She looked away and mumbled.

Nick wanted to wink at Allison, or give her a thumb-to-forefinger "okay" sign. That sounded like a fairly reasonable explanation, considering she had come up with it on the spur of the moment.

But Max was not so impressed. "Jeez!" he said. "Holy bejeesus. I don't know which one of you is the craziest. You kids been smoking something? Hot air balloons coming down from above. People hiring kids to spy on other people's laundry." He turned away and stalked toward the house.

"Sir," said Nick to his back. "What do you want us to do with the clothes?"

Max stopped but did not turn. "Fold them up and put them in the basket there." He pointed to an old wicker basket beside the back door and started to walk again.

"But, sir," said Nick.

Max smacked his hand to his forehead, sighed deeply and whispered, "What now?"

"What about the dog? Could you just throw the basket down?"

"Yeah! Sure!" He threw the basket behind him with one hand and opened the door with the other.

"Mr. Max," called Allison.

He stopped in the doorway.

"Should we take the clothes to the laundromat? Get them all clean and nice and bring them back? So Mrs. Max . . . so your wife won't be, you know, upset."

"No! Don't take anything anywhere. Except yourselves. Just take yourselves away from here. Bugger off." He slammed the door behind him.

Nick and Allison looked for labels as they folded laundry.

"It could be him," whispered Allison. "He seems to get mad easy. But we need more clues." She shook her head as she folded the last towel.

No labels saying *en Needle Club*. No list of names. Not on any of Max's laundry. At least not on any of the laundry hung out to dry that day. Too bad. It was a good plan except for that one little accident.

"Guess we can't find out about the razor just now, either. If he uses that kind. Or electric," said Allison

"Guess not," said Nick. "And I guess I better go talk to the police. Give them that burnt scrap of stuff." They jogged back to the road and grabbed their bikes.

"How about the book?" asked Allison. "Is it a clue they would want?"

"I don't know," said Nick. "We better ask."

"I wouldn't mind reading it. Unless you think it's important," said Allison.

"That's okay. Keep it for now. It didn't have anything to do with the fire, anyway. We'll see what they say about the label first."

"I have to get home right now," said Allison. "When should we go? To the police?"

Now that they had decided to turn in the evidence, Nick could hardly wait to get it over with. "I think right away. I'll go by myself."

Allison nodded. "Okay. That might be better, anyway. You found it."

They cycled home. Nick picked up the scrap of fabric and headed back to the RCMP station.

At first there didn't seem to be anybody in, but after a couple of minutes, a constable appeared in the doorway of the adjoining room, carrying a cup of coffee. There were only two policemen stationed on the island, and they soon became well known in the community, but Nick had never seen this one before. One of the regulars must be on holiday.

"When did you find this?" the policeman asked.

"The morning after the fire," said Nick. He was beginning to feel nervous.

The constable looked suddenly alert. He gazed at Nick for a second or two, then lifted the piece of fabric with a pair of tweezers from the desk where Nick had laid it and slipped it into an envelope. "Why didn't you report it sooner?" The policeman half-smiled at him, so his face looked friendly, but the words raised an alarm signal in Nick's head.

Could I be called an accessory after the fact, or something, for, for . . . concealing evidence, maybe?

"Well, because it was, um . . . quite a long way from the fire."

"Okay, son. You did the right thing, anyway." He was looking at a computer screen. "Your mother reported some vandalism, didn't she?"

Yikes! What else do they know about us?

"Yeah. A picture was wrecked," said Nick. He had thought he might tell about the scarecrow and the LEAVE OR DIE message, but he got a nervous kind of feeling that it might somehow be betraying his mother, to tell all that stuff without consulting her. They would put it on their computer, and it would look like his mother was the kind of person who had enemies, or something. And she was not.

Nick's brain tormented him as he rode home. Maybe he should have told about the other things, the scarecrow and the shaving cream. But what could they do? Protect his mother? How? They sure as heck were not going to put a bodyguard on her for the sake of what looked like kids' pranks.

Chapter 15

Nick's mother was back at work and feeling fine, and Jonathan went to Camp Laffalot under protest. It wasn't really a camp, just a day program put on by Parks and Rec. Nick was glad of Camp Laffalot; it meant he would not be called on to mind Jonathan.

"It's dumb. We don't laugh. Just the little kids do. They gargle," said Jonathan.

"You mean giggle," said his mother.

"Right. That's 'zactly what they do do."

However, when given the option of going to camp or shopping with Nick, Jonathan decided he could stand a few gargles after all.

Jim Price's birthday was coming up, and Nick was the gift shopper. The presents their dad had liked best during the past few years (not counting *The Book of Lists*, of course) were long-sleeved made-in-Canada all-cotton plaid shirts. He had said in a letter to Jonathan that they were the best jungle shirts he owned. So Nick and Jonathan decided that another shirt exactly like the old ones, only a different colour, would be a good present this year. Easy to mail, too.

"So," said Nick to Allison, "when I go to pick out the shirt for my dad I can look at the labels on all the clothes and maybe find the right one. And maybe that will help."

"Good," said Allison. "I have to stay home with my sisters. My folks are going to Vancouver. So while you're doing that, I'll read that book. The one you found. And, do you feel like . . . would you want to lend me your dad's letter? To read? About what you do with that stick to make it work? And I could figure out how we should try our own magic spell."

Nick did not want to tell Allison that the medicine stick was behind a pile of kindling in the woodshed. And he did not want to start fooling around with it anywhere near his house. What if it did have something to do with his mother getting sick, or all the other funny things around the place? Maybe they would get the mysteries solved before they had to use it. It was the last resort, in Nick's opinion.

The department store was in the same mall where Nick and Allison had had their first date. Though having a Coke together could not really be called a date, Nick liked to think of it that way.

Fourteen hours later, Nick could not get to sleep for thinking about the shopping trip.

Something *en Needle Club*. Or maybe something, something, *en Needle Club:* and a list of names. Nick thought his brain might get scrambled thinking about labels and *en Needle Club*, by the time he got back from town.

Labels. Jackets, shirts, sweaters, pants, vests, even underwear labels. He had seen them all. He had flipped through circular racks of bright fluorescent nylon squall jackets, dark Harris tweed and navy-blue flannel blazers, London Fog and Aquascutum topcoats. And pants: blue jeans, dress pants, full-cut, low-rise, medium-rise. Like looking for one particular paper clip in a high-rise office tower.

At first the store clerk had been helpful. "Looking for something in particular?"

Very particular, thought Nick. "Umm, just trying to get some ideas. For my dad's birthday," he said.

"We have a good buy on shirts. What size does he wear?" The man walked toward a tall stand made of plastic compartments, each one stuffed with folded packaged shirts.

Nick was examining a rack of dressing gowns.

"What size did you say?" The clerk's voice startled

Nick, and he almost bumped the man's nose as he turned his head suddenly.

"Umm, I'll just . . . ah, let you know if I find something." Nick moved to a table with a CLEARANCE: 50% OFF sign above it. This was even worse than looking for a paper clip. Each garment was different and they were jumbled together like somebody had just pulled them out of an enormous clothes dryer. Like looking for a blueberry under a huckleberry bush. The trouble was, he could spend forever looking under the wrong bush.

The underwear was easier. There were only five different brands, and that meant only five plastic-wrapped packages had to be squeezed and twisted so the labels were exposed.

There! A silver label! An artfully arranged rainbow of silk scarves on the wall. Just the edge of a label showing on the purple one. Nick held his breath. He couldn't reach high enough to touch the sliver of silver. He fumbled with the flower-like arrangement formed by the scarf ends. A tack popped out of the wall, and an emerald-green flower collapsed and turned into a wrinkled silk scarf end.

"We have others!" The voice sounded angry. Nick jerked his arm back and felt his elbow hit the man's stomach.

"Oof!" grunted the clerk.

"Sorry." Nick's face was hot.

"Excuse me? Excuse me?" A woman pulling a small boy by the hand tapped the clerk on the shoulder.

"In a hurry. Have to catch the bus. Do you mind? If I just ask one teensy question?" She looked at Nick. He shook his head.

"I'm thurs-dee," whined the little boy.

"These jackets." She pointed to a nearby rack. "Is that price . . . ." Her voice faded as she led the clerk away. The boy looked back over his shoulder and stuck his tongue out at Nick.

But where are the others? Where? Are? The? Others? Nick

looked around. There! A neatly folded stack of scarves lay in a square bin on top of a glove rack. He snatched the top one and pulled it open. Wrong side. He turned it over. His shoulders slumped. The silver label said *Giovanni Italian Designer Garments for the Discriminating Male. Made in Taiwan.* Might have known. What pyromaniac in his right mind would use a silk scarf to start a fire anyway?

Nick gave up at that point, and got on with the business of birthday-present buying. He found his father's favourite shirt brand, made by Bell Manufacturing, size medium, sleeve 34, in a muted grey and blue plaid. It was all sealed up in plastic, and the collar especially seemed perfect for his dad, the way it was shaped and held in place. The label was flat and neat against the neckband, not floppy or wrinkled, like some he had seen that afternoon.

"Well, you finally found something, I see," said the clerk as Nick attempted to hand over the shirt and two pairs of socks. "You'll have to take them to the cash register. See where that lineup is?" Nick saw where the lineup was, and tried not to feel too depressed as he waited to pay for his father's birthday gift.

The worst part was thinking about telling Allison. Geez! He should have gone swimming, or kayaking, or stayed home and helped her watch her sisters, or even gone skateboarding with Beaver and Grolinski. Better than spending half a day looking for a needle in a haystack.

Got "cliché" marked on my essay once for that. Needle in a haystack. Don't care. That's what it was. Exactly.

Chapter 16

Things weren't so bad really. The day was as bright as a tropical postcard and the chores were done. The dishes were washed, the petunias were watered, the laundry was folded and the patch of grass in front of the house was mowed. The bay shimmered and rippled in the sunshine. The sky was almost as blue as Allison's eyes, and the big arbutus tree in the front yard looked as though it were posing for a photograph.

Mom had gone to work again. Her flu really was better, and Jonathan had decided that there were a few laughs at Camp Laffalot after all.

It was a perfect day for kayaking. Kayaking with Allison. He should go ask her, but he didn't know how he could do that without actually going to their cabin and knocking on the door. And meeting her parents. Maybe he'd just walk down that way, act casual, play it by ear.

Mr. McKeghnie was sitting on a chair in front of one of the Taylor Bay Cottages reading a newspaper. No question about who it was, even from a distance. A white cast on his arm from wrist to elbow gleamed in the afternoon sun.

Nick took a deep breath, squared his shoulders and climbed up the twisting path from the beach. Just be calm, he coached himself. Calm and polite. Ask how his arm is. Say you're sorry it happened.

Geez! His brain had forgotten to watch his feet again. He was sprawled on the ground. One strong blackberry vine clutched his sock. Missy was barking like crazy and licking his face.

Mr. McKeghnie stood and looked in Nick's direction,

and a woman appeared in the cottage doorway.

Way to go Nick. Now the whole family knows you can do one thing. Fall down.

"Missy! Missy! Come here," called the woman. "Allison, come and get your dog."

Allison came leaping down the two front steps and grabbed Missy's collar. "Nick," she said and smiled, then turned suddenly serious. "Those blackberry vines are dangerous." She nodded at the tangle of bushes.

"Yeah," said Nick, as he jumped to his feet. "They just reach right out and whammo! You don't have a chance."

Allison laughed. Her father smiled, shook Nick's hand with his left one, said he was always glad to meet a friend of Allison's and went back to his newspaper. Her mother laughed, said that those vines really were a menace — she had almost tripped over them several times herself — and went back into the cabin.

How did I manage it? Instead of blushing I turned the whole thing into a joke. And Mr. McKeghnie called me a friend of Allison's.

"Allison would you like to cry tieracking?" he said.

"Pardon?" said Allison.

"Yo, Nick. Hey buddy." Two boys' voices called from the beach. *Oh no. Not Beaver and Grolinski.*

"Hey, Allison. Come and see the creature we found. It's awesome." Two girls' voices called from the water's edge.

"My sisters," said Allison, and shrugged.

"Those guys I know from school," said Nick, and shrugged. "I'll go and talk to them for a minute. Don't go away," he called over his shoulder.

Nick managed to convince Beaver and Grolinski that he had been trying to sell the McKeghnies a subscription to *The Flying Shingle.*

"How come? Since when?" asked Beaver.

"Since when what?" said Nick.

"Since when you been selling the island paper?"

"Well, I, ah . . . don't really *sell* it. But my mother has started to write some stuff for it. About the environment and stuff, so I . . . ah." He trailed off, looked down and squashed the bulb of a sea onion under his heel with a pop and a squirt.

"So who's your friend?" said Grolinski with a wink.

"Who?" Nick tried to make his face look blank.

"The girl. The female of the species." He nodded toward Allison.

"Search me," said Nick. "Hey listen, guys, I've got to go."

"Aw, c'mon, c'mon, c'mon, c'mon," said Grolinski. "We're going to hang out at the park. See what's to be seen — you know." He winked again. "Hot weather. Bikinis."

"No thanks," said Nick. "I have to go home and write a letter to my dad. And wrap his birthday present. I promised my mother I'd rake the yard, and she needs kindling, and . . . ."

"Kindling?" Beaver looked puzzled. "Hasn't she noticed? It's the hottest day of the year."

Nick shrugged. "Yeah. Well. Sometimes she likes to light the wood stove, makes the room look nice, and . . . ."

"You turning into some kind of geek, or what?" said Grolinski. "You never want to do guy stuff anymore."

Nick managed to convince his buddies that he was not turning into a geek, that he still did want to do guy stuff — some other day — and that his mother did occasionally light a fire in the wood stove in the middle of summer, so they could toast marshmallows. Because of outdoor fires being banned, and all that.

He also managed to get the words straight and invite Allison to try kayaking.

They marched along the gravel road, elbows bent, Nick's red kayak gleaming overhead. Nick could hear Allison's voice singing behind him, "*En roulant ma boule roulant.*"

Nick did not sing. Not right then. He might sing again

one day, but not then. Especially not when Allison could hear. His voice, like his feet, didn't always do what he wanted it to do. Sometimes it would surprise him and come out much higher or lower than he intended. And that was not the worst of it. The worst of it was when it changed its mind and went from high to low and back again in a single sentence. Or even a single word.

"Which beach, *ma boule roulant*," sang Allison as they neared the bottom of the hill.

"Pilot Bay." Nick turned left as he spoke. Taylor Bay, across the small neck of land, was sunnier in the afternoons, but if Beaver and Grolinski came back to this end of the island to do "guy" stuff on the beach, they would probably be doing it there. Better stick to Pilot.

They set the kayak on the sand. Allison peeled off her shorts and T-shirt, folded them and placed them on a log. Then she bent over, unbuckled her sandals, set them beside the clothing and wiggled her toes in the sand.

Allison's bathing suit was a brilliant blue. It and the red kayak were the most startling colours on the landscape. Nick tried not to stare. She looked terrific in the blue bathing suit. His lips felt funny and his skin tingled. He swallowed twice.

"Here we are. The Timex Two. I guess we should think about what to do next," said Allison. "About solving the crimes."

"Later. Let's kayak now and talk later. Okay?"

"Okay." She smiled and hopped on one foot like a little girl playing hopscotch.

The hard part was yet to come. Nick had to take off his jeans and then *she* would see *him* in a bathing suit. His long skinny legs. His too-big feet.

Maybe I could just keep my pants on. Take off my shirt.

He did. He didn't mind his body from the waist up. His shoulders were square and his upper arms were muscular from kayaking. He even had a few black hairs on his chest.

Allison was bending down and touching her toes and counting. "*Un, deux, trois, quatre, cinque* . . . ."

Nick took off his jeans and pretended his legs didn't exist while he waded into the water with the kayak. He steadied it while Allison got in.

He swam out into the bay and she criss-crossed back and forth beside him.

"Hold the paddle at right angles. Dip it straight down. Pull. Right, left, right, left. Straight up," he called to her above the splash of waves, the cries of gulls and the other beach sounds around them: people talking, children laughing and motorboats roaring their way out to the open sea.

Nick wished he had a movie camera to take pictures of Allison. Her expression changed so rapidly. One second she looked nervous, her eyes wide, her mouth set in a straight line; the next minute her tongue was clamped over her upper lip as she concentrated. Then she laughed aloud and her face sparkled as she got control over the little boat.

"It's fun, Nick. It feels like riding on a kite. Except it does what I want." She leaned toward him and almost tipped over. "Once I learn how." She struggled with the paddle. Nick swam a few strokes to help her, but she was doing fine. "You have to concentrate all the time, don't you?" she laughed. "Want a turn? It would be fun to try a kayak for two sometime. Both of us together."

"Yeah. We've got one. We could, sometime, maybe." Nick wasn't sure how he would feel about going out in the big kayak with Allison. The one that belonged to him and his father. He decided to leave that thought for later and just concentrate on using the small one. "Want to try riding it while I paddle?" he said.

"Can you do that?" She looked surprised. "I've never seen anybody do that."

"It's tricky. But possible."

"Can you do it?"

"Yeah. But the paddler has to be pretty, ah . . . experienced."

He didn't want to hurt her feelings, but he knew he would not be able to ride the kayak with her paddling. She wasn't good enough yet. "You want to try? I'll paddle," he said.

Nick swam and Allison paddled back to shore and they changed places.

"Swim up behind it, over the back end. Lie flat on your stomach, and wrap your arms around it, like, like . . . climbing a tree, only horizontal instead of vertical." Nick gestured with his own arms. "This really takes concentration. Both of us have to be perfect."

Nick kept his attention riveted on maintaining his balance as he felt the kayak lunge and sway under Allison's weight. Dip, pull. Dip, pull. Concentrate. Mind and body focused.

She was doing it! She was settled on the kayak. He could feel the extra weight. He pulled harder and closed his eyes for a second to keep focused on the dip and pull.

"Nick!" Her laughing voice behind him, "this is . . . ." Water whooshed over his body and closed over his head. He popped his head up and looked around.

Allison's wet hand touched his shoulder. "Sorry," she sputtered and coughed. "I raised my head to talk to you, and . . . man overboard!"

"That's okay. Happens all the time."

They righted the kayak and took turns bailing with a plastic bottle cut away down one side for the purpose. They smiled and spluttered and laughed at each other. Allison sang "Row row, row your boat" and wanted Nick to sing rounds with her. Singing was out of the question for him, so he recited "The Song My Paddle Sings."

They fooled around in the water, righting the kayak, bailing it out, reciting poetry and singing songs. Allison was like a cork. Bet she couldn't sink if she tried, thought Nick.

"Should we stop now and do some Timex Two stuff?" asked Allison.

"Naah. Later." Nick wished the kayaking lessons could go on forever.

Allison tried to ride the back again. Twice more they overturned. Twice more they bailed. They got it perfect in the end. Two bodies in perfect balance on the kayak. His arm and shoulder muscles strained with the pull of the paddle.

Allison sang with her head under water, getting Nick to guess which song it was. He didn't guess right. Even if he *had* known he wouldn't have said, because every time he was wrong she put her hands on his shoulders, thrust her water-speckled face toward him and said "Gottcha." Her long hair, turned darker, clung to her shoulders and floated around her upper arms.

Silly games. Songs and verses and guessing what somebody was saying under water. He had done that with Beaver and Grolinski at the age of six. But they didn't seem silly now. Not with Allison. They seemed light-hearted and funny. Hilarious, in fact.

They carried the kayak between them and leaned it against the giant cedar tree that overhung the beach at Pilot Bay. They lay back on the sand and watched the cedar boughs pattern the blue sky, and the daisy-petal clouds drift over the mainland mountains.

"What a perfect day," said Allison.

"Yeah." Nick couldn't remember a more perfect one. They were both exhausted. The sand was warm. The air was thick and heavy with the smell of seaweed and the hum of voices of the other beach-goers.

"I guess we should talk now. About solving the mysteries." Her voice sounded husky and low, as though she were half asleep.

"What mysteries? I don't know anything about any mysteries." Nick turned his head toward her and smiled a lazy smile.

"Strange, about that book," said Allison and sat up

suddenly. Some urgency in her voice made Nick's stomach flip. He sat up.

"What? What's strange?"

"Well, funny things happen. You know, it kind of reminds me of the things that have happened here. A doll is strangled. A picture is wrecked, not a photograph, but a portrait. You know, a painted picture of a person. And a dance hall is burned down. I get this weird feeling when I'm reading it. Like I almost know what's going to happen next."

"Have you finished it?" Nick felt a knot of worry start to form in his stomach.

"No. It kind of gives me the creeps. I'm not sure I want to know what happens next. But I guess we should find out. Shouldn't we?"

"Yeah. I guess."

"Oh, one different thing," said Allison. "A car is shoved over the edge of a parkade, onto the street below."

A car pushed over the edge? Nick's worry knot clenched in a quick spasm.

"What's the matter, Nick?" Allison's voice was close to his ear. "You shivered."

"Oh. Just thinking about that day. You were there. The day my mom's car almost fell off the ferry."

"Oh, right." Allison's forehead was furrowed and she stared into the distance. "I forgot about that. Or didn't connect it with your mother."

"What if somebody pushed it?" They both spoke at once.

"It's something else to add to the list," said Nick. He picked up a broken seashell and tossed it at a log.

"Don't be discouraged, Nick." She put her hand on his arm and leaned close. "We'll solve it. We will. I got it all figured out. How we can do the magic spell. Let's try it."

"I don't know." said Nick. "I just hope . . . ."

"Hope what?"

"That . . . oh, nothing."

"Come on, tell me. We're The Timex Two, remember.

Keep on ticking," said Allison.

"Just . . . ." He stared at his thumbnail for a second and then rubbed it with his other thumb. "That my mom is okay. You know. That there isn't some weirdo really out to get her."

"Yeah. Nick, we've got to watch, really watch. Use our brains."

"That's what I keep thinking." Nick scratched his head.

"And if all else fails . . . ." Allison left the sentence unfinished.

"Yeah?"

"We'll try the stick. The magic."

Chapter 17

"I thought we had some of that nice paper left." Nick was sitting at the kitchen table looking through a box of gift wrap and ribbons. "You know — the one with the sailboats on it."

"Oh, sorry. Jonnie used it last February for valentines." His mother took a sip of sherry from a small stemmed glass, then set it down on the table and turned the page of a book.

"Valentines! Valentines? What have boats got to do with valentines?" said Nick irritably.

"Lots." Jonathan stuck out his chin. He was standing in the doorway between the kitchen and the living room. Cartoon character voices came from the television set behind him. "'Will you sail away with me and be my valentine?' That's what I put on them."

"Geez!" said Nick. "How many girls did you invite to sail away?"

"Not just girls. I sent valentines to boys, too. Everybody in my class, and in Beavers, and some little kids in kindergarten, and . . . ."

"Oh, never mind." Nick smoothed out some plain white tissue paper and placed the new plaid shirt in the centre of it.

"Bell Shirt. Made in, *Fabrique au*, Canada," he read the shirt label aloud.

"They're made in Belleville, that's why they're called Bell," said his mother.

The label was neat and flat-looking. Nick tilted the plastic package under the light to have a better look at it. The bottom edge didn't look the same as the sides. They were kind of crimped, but the bottom was perfectly smooth and . . . *folded?*

Nick pulled the bag open and slid the shirt out. He turned the label up.

He gasped. The hair on the back of his neck prickled. A shiver ran down his spine and his stomach did a little flip-flop. Embroidered on the back of the folded Bell shirt label were the words *Golden Needle Club* followed by thirty names. The printing was very small and ran diagonally across the fabric.

The label I found at the community hall fire is like the kind on my father's favourite shirt? But this label was not silver, it was plain grey.

"What's the matter, Nick?" His mother looked up.

"Nothing. I just wondered why it has Golden Needle Club and all these names on the back here." He handed the shirt to her.

"I guess it must be a way of honouring long-time employees. Good idea, too. To encourage pride in workmanship. Jonathan!" She called toward the living room. "Will you please turn that noise down?"

"You forgot an 'I' message, Mom," Jonathan called back.

"When you turn the volume up so loud I can't hear myself think. I would like you to turn it down."

"Hear yourself think? Hear yourself think? How can you hear thinking? How can you . . . ?" Jonathan was back in the doorway.

"Oh, it's just an expression."

"Like a busy bird in the bush equals . . . What is it?"

"A bird in the hand is worth two in the bush," she said with a sigh.

"You mean like people who live in grass houses shouldn't stow thrones, or . . . ."

"Yes, Jonathan. People who live in glass houses shouldn't throw stones, a stitch in time saves nine, children should be seen and not heard, I can't hear myself think. They're aphorisms, sayings, proverbs. Now will you please turn down the volume!"

Nick could hear himself think and he didn't like what he was hearing.

One of my dad's shirts? Used to start a fire? But my dad is in the jungle. They set fires in the jungle, too. Some people do. Maybe it's black magic. Maybe the medicine stick could somehow . . . . Aw, get real, Nick. Be sensible. Other people besides Dad wear plaid shirts.

But why was the label not silver, like the burnt one he had found? Maybe they stopped using silver now. Maybe . . . yeah, probably this was cheaper. Plain grey cloth. Everything else about it was identical. Same kind of embroidery, even a lot of the same names.

Thomas Turner wears tartan shirts. And Thomas Turner writes murder stories. And Thomas Turner's book was there, where the bulldozer crashed. Allison says it has a lot of stuff in it the same as what really happened. And if anybody saw Thomas Turner skulking around where he had no reason to be, they would just think he was looking for ideas for his books. Maybe Allison was right. Why didn't I listen to her, when she wanted to put a tail on Thomas Turner?

"Are you worried about something, Nick?" asked his mother. She got up from the table and carried her glass to the sink. "It's a nice present. I'm sure he'll like those colours."

"No, no. The present is fine."

But I'm scared, I don't want to know that maybe one of my father's shirts was soaked in gasoline and . . . .

Should he tell her? He looked at his mother's face. It was pale and drawn-looking, and she seemed to have lost weight. Her hair didn't shine with its usual glints of gold. Nick felt a clutch of love mixed with fear in the pit of his stomach.

Something bad was going to happen to his mother. It had already started.

Black magic, or voodoo, or just malicious threats from

a real live human being — Nick didn't care about the cause. All he wanted to do right then was get away from it. Get his mother away. Protect her from the awful doom he felt certain was coming.

"Let's move. To town," he said.

"I thought you liked living here. I think it's worth the effort, island living. I know it's hard sometimes, with the ferry, and . . . ." She stopped speaking and moved to stand in front of him. "You're worried about the threats, aren't you? The phone call, and the picture, and my good blouse ripped? Nick." She put her hand on his shoulder. "It's nothing to worry about — just somebody trying to scare me away from the logging issue, probably. Try not to worry. I won't react to threats, Nick. I will not!" She shook her head and leaned down to look into his eyes.

Chapter 18

Nick's mother had a relapse the next morning. She was too weak and tired to get out of bed.

"The flu can be like that," she said. "You think it's gone and then it flares up again. I'll be fine. All I need is rest."

Nick didn't think that rest was all his mother needed. He wished he could get her away from the island. But since that was impossible, the only other thing he could think to do was to watch her. Stay near the house all the time. Watch for any strangers wandering nearby. And make sure there were no chances for somebody to do something horrible to a picture, or her car, or *her*.

Jonathan was invited to a birthday party — a swim at the big pool in Nanaimo and lunch at MacDonald's. Nick was glad he didn't have to go. Lunch at MacDonald's with eleven seven- and eight-year-olds was not his idea of a good time. Lunch almost anywhere with Allison would be a different matter. But he couldn't go to Allison's and stay home and guard his mother at the same time. Why hadn't he just asked Allison to come to his home?

Because you're still a wimp, Nick. Might as well admit it. You're a wimp around girls. Just because Allison treats you like a winner doesn't make you one. She hasn't got anybody else to hang around with over here.

But Nick did get his wish — he had lunch with Allison. There was a firm knock at the back door at 10:30, and there she stood, smiling, wearing navy shorts and a white T-shirt with a white collar and a small sprig of forget-me-nots embroidered on the pocket. Nick liked the look of the little blue flowers on her shirt.

"I'm glad you came," said Nick. Then the old feelings

came back. He felt awkward and shy and turned away so
she wouldn't see him blush. "I'll just go and see if my
mother wants anything. Want to go out on the deck?"

Nick's mother was asleep in her bedroom.

He sat on the sun deck with Allison and unwrapped
his father's birthday present to show her the label. No
question about it. It was exactly the same as the one he
had turned in to the police, except this one was grey and
not silver, and it smelled new and cardboardy. He
wrapped the shirt up again, but the paper was more crin-
kled than ever now. Allison helped with the folding of the
corners and the sticky tape, and when they finished, it
looked quite all right.

Sitting in the sunshine, looking at the moving ripples
on the bay, smelling the salt water and sea-creature scents
that filled the air and listening to Allison's calm voice
began to melt the black fear in Nick's stomach.

"I wonder what your mother did with your father's
old shirts? You know, after he left?" said Allison.

"I don't know. But I guess somebody could have got
hold of one of Dad's old shirts, all right. Good thinking,
Allison." He put his hand briefly on her arm. She looked at
him and smiled and he didn't blush.

If he could just not think about blushing. But thinking
about not thinking about blushing made it happen. He was
glad that Allison was watching two windsurfers, both in the
water, trying to pull their sails erect.

Allison took a deep breath, stretched her arms above her
head and then wrapped them around her shoulders. "Let's
try that magic stick, Nick. This afternoon."

"Okay. Sure." Nick wasn't too sure about using the
stick, but Allison's face looked bright and confident. "Maybe
we could try it. Later. Oh, you know what? We forgot to get
the mail yesterday. But I don't want to leave my mom alone."

"I can get it if you want," said Allison. "I have to go and
tell my mother I'm having lunch at your house anyway."

Nick went to the woodshed, half-expecting the medicine stick to have disappeared, or changed somehow, but it seemed as familiar as the old green watering can that sat on top of the stacked wood. As he lifted it down, it seemed to fit just right into his hand. Both sides of the stone face looked soft, almost like they were absorbing the sunshine. A mouse or some other creature had nibbled a little hole in the straw binding, which proved that it wasn't evil, didn't it? He carried it back, laid it on the sun deck and arranged the feathers in a fan. Then he smiled at it, and it smiled back.

He heated a tin of consommé for his mother.

Allison arrived back just as he was putting dill pickles on the plates beside two grilled cheese sandwiches. She handed him the mail and he sorted through it quickly. "This one's not for us. It's for Uncle Hay — got put in the wrong box. Come on. Let's eat. The sandwiches are getting cold."

They sat on the wide shallow steps that led from the deck to the little patch of grass between the house and the bank. Nick was hungry, and had swallowed the last bite of his sandwich before Allison had started her second half. "I'm going to get bread and peanut butter. Want some?" he said as he stood.

"No thanks. These are delicious, Nick." Allison tipped up her glass of milk. "You sure know how to make good grilled cheese. Oh, Nick," she called.

He was already through the patio door and he stopped and turned. "Yeah?"

"How about getting the letter, the one about how to do magic, while you're in there?" She pointed with her chin toward the house.

"Sure. Okay." Nick was still not convinced that he wanted to fool around with black magic. But still, it wouldn't hurt to just read the instructions again, with Allison.

"Oh, I asked my mom about Dad's old shirts," he said as he came back carrying a sandwich, two cookies and a letter.

Allison swallowed, and looked up. "So what did she

say. About the shirts?"

"Oh, she gave them away. To anybody who wanted them. And the leftovers she took to the Salvation Army." He flopped down beside her and handed her the letter.

"Hmm," said Allison. She unfolded the page and smoothed it carefully on her knees. "Let's see now. We need a quiet place, a building of some kind. We need two people to do the spell. We face each other and place our hands alternately around the medicine stick handle. I guess that means like playing *one potato, two potato?*" She looked at Nick questioningly. Her face was animated, like she was a little girl learning how to play a new game.

Nick nodded. He was beginning to think this might not be a bad idea after all. Allison seemed sure about it. "We've got an old fort," he said. "Just back up there." He pointed across the back yard to a stand of tall fir trees behind the garden.

"You have?" Allison looked excited. "Well, it must be private. I haven't seen it. Let's check it out."

"Sure," said Nick. "We can see the house from there. We made sure of that when we built it. We could see people coming, but nobody could see us."

"Neat," said Allison. "Let's go. Oh, no . . . wait a minute."

Nick was stretching, getting ready to stand up.

"Let's see the rest of the instructions first." She turned the page over, and leaned toward it.

The rest of the instructions talked about pointing the stick in all four directions and chanting to the gods. Nick's father said he was sorry he didn't know what words were supposed to be used. He couldn't understand the language. But he did see the holders of the medicine stick turn three times to the right, three times to the left and then shake it hard.

"So we'll have to make up the chanting part," said Allison. "And we have to get in the mood . . . you know, like a trance. So close your eyes and meditate." She immediately closed her own and cradled her hands together on her lap.

They sat in silence. Nick did not close his eyes, but he did try to think peaceful thoughts. It was another sunny day. Of course, having Allison there made it a lot nicer than usual. Across the bay a huge flock of crows all headed for the same tree. A hummingbird's plumage shone like fluorescent paint as it hovered over a pink petunia that cascaded down from a pot on an old stump near the woodshed, just ten feet from where they were sitting. It was as quiet and peaceful as ever, except . . . .

Magic! This could not be happening. He was sitting on his own sun deck and he and Allison were actually going to start fooling around with magic?

Allison carried the medicine stick with one hand, waving it slowly back and forth in front of her as she picked her way along the path through the trees and brush beside the Prices' driveway. The stick did look magic, in a nice friendly way, when Allison carried it like that. She looked like a priestess or a goddess leading a procession to a temple, thought Nick. He should be carrying a candle, but a candle wouldn't make much of a showing in the middle of a hot sunny afternoon.

The fort smelled of old wood and rotting leaves and sweet wild berry wine. It really was a wonderfully private and quiet place.

"You're right. You can see the driveway and the house from here." Allison spoke softly as she stooped to peer through an old ship's porthole in the wall. That wall had more different kinds of wood in it than a beach has seashells. Driftwood, discarded shingles, left-over fence boards, a bamboo tray, part of an old chest, a picture frame, kindling and cedar floorboards from an old cabin were nailed, tied, propped and wired together in a haphazard way. It had seemed the most beautiful design in the world when Nick and his friends had built it five summers earlier.

Age had improved its looks. Moss and fir cones and arbutus leaves covered the roof. Blackberry vines and honeysuckle climbed the walls. Salal and Oregon grape hugged the corners, and an old rotted stump guarded the entrance.

"But it's not very high. We're supposed to hold the stick up high, and . . . ." Allison stood and looked around. "It's so nice in here. It's such a perfect place. It feels like the right place."

It did seem like the right place. Nick could hear the rustle of leaves and the hum of insects, the whisper of a loose strip of cedar bark brushing against an outside wall, the thump of his heart.

"So, let's salute the gods of creation," said Allison. "Sun, moon, water and earth. We'll sing, umm . . . let's see. We'll sing 'gods of creation, we salute you.' And point the stick each direction — north, south, east, west.

"Here. I put my left hand on the handle, you put your left one just above it. That's it. Now my right. And your right." There was just barely enough room on the short handle for four hands squeezed close together.

They were standing in the middle of the small hut.

"Now, what we'll do is raise it up as high as we can, and just touch each of the four walls. And chant."

They stood side by side and faced the eastern wall, the stick between them. "God of creation, we salute you. God of the sunlight, make us wise." Allison's eyes were half-closed and she drew the words out into a long chant, as their four hands lowered the stick so the feathers brushed the wall. A small feather fragment floated loose and clung to the wall near the corner.

"Now south, for water," whispered Allison, and turned to the southern wall, the one closest to the ocean. "This one is a goddess." She looked at Nick sternly.

He suspected that she had just that moment decided that they must have goddesses, as well as gods, but the magic did seem to be working. The forest outside was hushed. A streak of sunshine quivered in Allison's long hair, making it look like a waterfall.

"Goddess of creation, we salute you. Goddess of the waters, make us wise." Nick half-closed his eyes and joined the chant as they slowly lowered the stick. The long feathers flowed and curved like a swimming fish. The dark wood of the wall glowed with red and then faded again.

The small feather clinging to the eastern wall fluttered in the draft caused by the moving stick.

"The earth is a goddess, too."

"Okay," he whispered, and turned with her to face west.

"Goddess of creation, we salute you. Goddess of the earth, make us wise." Nick watched closely for the wall to glow, but it wasn't red. This time the colour was bronze, like a buried fire.

One more turn. One more chant.

"God of creation, we salute you. God of the moonlight, make us wise." A silver glow. Impossible. Or maybe it was because the wood was different. It reflected different colours. Yeah, that was it. Different kind of wood.

Allison was looking into his eyes. "Now we hold it up. Turn three times to the left, three times to the right, shake it hard and watch where the feathers point."

In a dream, Nick turned with Allison. Her hands, made into fists around the stick, felt solid and soft at the same time, and the blackberry smell was sweet and heavy. Allison's face changed with reflections of pink and red and blue as a streak of sunlight danced on the turning plumage.

"Now shake it," whispered Allison.

They held the stick up and shook it hard. Nick felt something. Energy from Allison's two hands? It felt real. Like a warm current of some kind.

"Oh spirit of the feathers, lead us to the evil one." Allison stared hard at the stick. "The feathers don't seem to be pointing anywhere. Do they?"

"Un-Un. No. They don't." Nick shook his head. The

feathers were settling themselves lightly around the stone face in perfect symmetry.

"Too bad." Allison's head drooped and her shoulders slumped. "Oh, well. We'll try again, later. Let's get your list and use our brains instead. Magic spells don't seem to be the answer right now."

Trust her. If one thing didn't work, try something else. What a girl!

A twig cracked suddenly and Allison jumped. The sound snapped Nick's attention away from magic and back to the worry about his mother. "Just the heat. They snap like that in the heat," he said. "Better check on my mom." He scrambled around the old stump and flailed his way down the path, across the back yard and into the house.

She was fine. She was sitting in a chair in her bedroom doing embroidery. It looked funny. To see his mother doing embroidery. She didn't seem like the embroidery type.

"How come you're doing that?" he asked. "I didn't think you liked that kind of stuff much."

"Once in a while I do. It's very relaxing," she said and looked up at him. "You're out of breath." She pulled the thread taut.

"Yeah. I just, ah, raced Allison down the driveway. She stopped to look at the fort."

"Oh."

"Just give a yell, if you need anything, Mom. I'll be out on the deck."

"Thanks, Nick. But I won't need anything I can't get for myself. I really am feeling much better. I think I've got it beat this time. Whatever bacteria or virus it happened to be."

"Is she okay?" Allison walked toward him across the yard.

Nick nodded.

"I left the medicine stick up there. In the very middle of the back wall. So it can get its act together. Then we'll go try it again. We should be in a real trance, you know. That's what they do. How do you think we could *really* get into a trance?" Allison stared absent-mindedly at Nick and frowned.

Allison read Nick's list. He was glad he had made a new one, in his neatest printing, as she held it in both hands and rocked back and forth and read aloud.

"Wednesday, July 21st. Car almost fell off the ferry. Monday, August 9th, loggers tried to start logging; the scarecrow was choked; wire strung in the trees and my dad got a broken wrist.

"Tuesday, August 10th, the bulldozer crashed over the cliff . . . saw Max running away from the scene of the crime.

"Wednesday, August 11th, found Thomas Turner's book."

"Hold it!" said Nick.

"Huh?" Allison turned to look at him.

"Remember when you opened it. The feather?" Nick was talking fast. "Feathers. When you opened that book there was a feather . . . ."

"Huh? Oh, right. A feather floated out. I forgot about that."

"And Max has chickens. And . . . ."

"Ni-ick." Allison dropped the list, jumped to her feet, grabbed both of his hands and pulled him up.

"Come on!" She was running toward the path to the fort and motioning for him to follow.

"What?" he called after her.

"Look." Allison was standing in the doorway of the fort, pointing. The small piece of red feather was still clinging to the wall, only now it glistened and quivered because the sun had moved and the streak of sunlight was focused directly on it.

"Geez! It does seem to be trying to tell us something. But what?"

Allison raised her arm and pointed straight at the feather. "Who lives there. That way?"

"What do you mean? Oh, umm. Well, Thomas Turner lives over that way."

"Thomas Turner does, does he?"

"And Thomas Turner wears tartan shirts. Maybe he did have something to do with it after all," said Nick.

"And Thomas Turner's book was there, at the scene of the crime." Allison's arm was around his shoulder.

"And you said the things that happened in his book are quite a bit the same as here." Nick's arm was around Allison's waist. "I thought he couldn't be doing the things he wrote about . . . but, you know . . . maybe he's so smart that's what he'd think other people would think. Maybe the stick is trying to tell us something."

"Come on!" Allison dropped her arm, grabbed his hand and led him down the path, talking excitedly over her shoulder. "We'll make a plan. On the deck. Close to your mom. Maybe the stick did work. Maybe this is it, Nick. Maybe The Timex Two are going to solve it. Have to find evidence."

"But don't say anything in front of my mom." Nick pulled on Allison's hand.

"No." Allison stopped and Nick bumped into her, then stepped back quickly, dropped her hand and blushed. But she wasn't looking at him. She was standing with the palm of her hand against her forehead and muttering, "We'll act like everything is normal. Keep thinking . . . . A plan."

Nick's mother had moved out onto the deck and was reclining on a lounge, still embroidering. She did look better. Her cheeks were pink and her lips didn't look so pinched and thin. Her hair didn't shine as much as usual, though, and her hands shook a little as she threaded a needle. But she did look better, and she sounded better, too.

"It's so nice to meet you, Allison. Sorry to hear about what happened to your father. That sort of activity is unforgivable, absolutely unforgivable, endangering life and limb like that — wire strung in the trees. I certainly hope that the culprit is caught. I wouldn't mind a cup of tea, Nick. If you feel like making one?" She set her embroidery on the small table beside her, stretched and leaned back.

"Sure." Nick moved toward the door.

"Thanks, Nick. You're a good guy." His mother smiled at him.

"I'll help." Allison followed.

They carried a loaded tray back out, then sat on the deck. They drank tea and ate toast and talked and laughed. Nick felt warm and happy watching his mother and Allison smile at each other. Then he remembered why he was sitting at home on the sun deck instead of skateboarding with Beaver and Grolinski, or picking blackberries for the freezer or, choice number one, kayaking with Allison.

He shivered and glanced around the yard. Paper-thin red bark curled back from the trunk of the arbutus tree, leaving exposed green patches. Usually Nick liked the way it looked — it made him think of Indians inventing birchbark canoes and of Egyptians making papyrus. Now it just looked like blotches on the tree's skin.

"Good toast. Thanks, Allison." Nick's mother took another slice from the plate Allison passed.

Gravel scrunched on the driveway, a car door slammed, the back door banged and Jonathan came whooping out. He was wearing a pirate hat and carrying a rubber sword. "Ahoy, all you land lovers," he said, brandishing the sword in the air. He stopped with a skid in front of Allison. "Who are you? Are you Allison?"

"It's lubbers," said his mother.

"I thought it was Allison."

"Yes, that is Allison. And its landlubbers, not land lovers."

"And you must be Long John Silver," said Allison. "Also known as Jonathan Price. I'm very pleased to meet you." She held out her hand. Jonathan stared at her face, then at her hand. The sword dropped to the deck floor with a bounce and he solemnly shook her hand up and down vigorously.

"Are you a slick chick? Do you know what a dorky airhead is? Do you like heavy metal? Will you teach me to jive? Who moved my *Mad*?" All of these questions were directed to Allison, who smiled, then laughed and shook her head.

"No, I am not a slick chick. A dorky airhead is a jerk. No, I do not like heavy metal. Sure, I'll teach you jive sometime. And there's your magazine, on the table."

"No, not that one. My new one. Who moved my new one?"

"It's right there where you left it. On the floor by the sideboard," said his mother. "When you leave your things lying around like that I either have to pick them up or look at an untidy room, and I feel annoyed." She crossed her ankles, clasped her hands at the back of her head and leaned back against the lounge.

"Mother. Come *on*." It was the same tone of voice Jonathan used when he was trying to persuade ants to travel the new highway he had scraped out for them in the dirt. "I left it *prezactly* there, where it was before. Somebody turned it to a different page. And wrinkled it. And stepped on it. And . . . ."

"Geez!" said Nick. "How do you know? You came roaring through there like a bat out of . . . I mean, like a tornado. Don't try to tell me you saw all that."

"I did too." Jonathan ran into the house and came back waving the magazine. "Somebody moved it. I wish people wouldn't tell fibhoods."

"Falsehoods," said his mother.

Allison was sitting on the steps. She turned sideways and looked as though she was trying not to laugh. She stood. "I think I should go home. Thanks for the lunch. And tea." She looked at Nick.

"Thank you, Allison, for coming over," said Patricia. "It's been lovely to meet you."

"You too." Allison waved. She started toward the corner of the house and Nick jumped up to follow her.

"Oh, Allison." Nick's mother sorted through the stack of mail on the table beside her and waved an envelope aloft. "Maybe you wouldn't mind just dropping this letter off to Haylett on your way past. That little brown house, just across . . . ."

"Sure. Okay. I know which house."

"I'll give it to her." Jonathan grabbed the letter from his mother and jumped off the deck in one leap. "Good bye." He held out his hand for another handshake.

Nick followed Allison and watched her get on her bicycle.

"What do we do now?" she asked. She was balanced with one foot on the ground and the other on the bike pedal. She flipped her head so her hair swirled away from the back of her neck. "About solving the mystery."

"One thing we have to do is find out what brand of shirt Thomas Turner wears," said Nick. He walked beside her while she pedalled slowly up the driveway.

"So we have to find out what brand of shirt he wears. And if he uses that squirting kind of shaving cream. And, and . . . you know I keep thinking about Max's chickens. Could that feather be pointing to Max's house, too?" asked Allison.

"No, not really. Well, yes, I guess it could. He lives sort of over that way. And feathers, and chickens, and shaving cream could all be him. And tartan shirts. I haven't seen him wear any, but then he's usually wearing his ferry uniform. And he sure has plenty of gas around his place, for working on those old cars. I guess we should really try to sleuth the both of them."

"You could invite him over for tea. Thomas Turner, I mean," said Allison. "And check out his shirt somehow. All English people have tea, so . . . ." They had reached the top of the driveway, and Allison got off her bike and held it steady with one hand on the handlebar.

"But won't that seem kind of funny?" Nick shook his

head. "We've never invited him for tea before."

"Then let's think of a good reason for doing it now," said the practical Allison.

"I know. I'll say I'm a big murder mystery fan and I'm writing a story of my own, and then I'll ask him to drop in for tea on Saturday. 'Cause Mom will be home from work that day, for sure. Do I have to say tea? Can't I say a Coke, or lemonade or something?"

"Sure. And I'll spill lemonade on his shirt. And he'll have to take it off. And The Timex Two will get the goods on him. Or maybe not." Allison sighed and stared at the ground and nudged a pebble with her toe. "I still keep thinking about Max," she said.

"Yeah. We have to have a good look around his place. For more clues. And his shirts — maybe he got one of my dad's old shirts at a garage sale, or something. The dog knows us now, and we can take him something — a bone or a . . . whatever dogs like."

Allison's head jerked erect and she stared into space. "What was that?"

"What?" whispered Nick.

"I thought I heard a noise. Shhhhh." She held a finger to her lips.

Nick strained to listen. Was there a rustle in the bushes?

"Can't hear anything," he whispered.

"Just the wind, I guess. Sorry. I'm getting kind of jumpy." Allison shook herself and took a deep breath. "So, I could ride around that way on my way home. Past Max's place. Pretend I'm lost and ask directions. Maybe find out in a roundabout way what shift he works tomorrow," she said. "And I'll find out the dog's name. Pretend I'm crazy about dogs, you know, and just want to know what his name is. That should help."

"He'll remember you from the clothesline," warned Nick.

Chapter 19

Nick could hear the clack of typewriter keys as he approached the little cabin hidden in the woods where Thomas Turner "retreated" to do his writing. He stood outside for several minutes trying to get enough courage to knock on the door. Maybe Thomas Turner would be furious at being interrupted at his work. Yes. He would be furious. Nick turned away and started home.

But what would he tell Allison? She'd be sure to keep her part of the bargain — stop at Max's and pretend she was crazy about barking dogs.

Knock on the door fast, before you have time to think about it.

The typewriter's click stopped and Nick could hear a chair scraping on a wooden floor.

"Good afternoon, old chap." Thomas's shirt cuffs were unbuttoned and folded back and he wore little half-glasses perched on his nose.

"Good afternoon, Mr. Turner. My name is Nicholas Price, and . . . ." He stopped. Thomas was staring over Nick's left shoulder as though he could see something strange.

"I beg your pardon? Sorry." He tilted his head back and peered at Nick through his little glasses.

"My name is Nicholas Price."

"Quite so. To be sure." Thomas Turner was staring over Nick's shoulder into space again.

"I live just over there, on Decourcey Drive, and I really dig, I mean like, mysteries."

"Yes. Yes." He looked back at Nick.

"Especially yours. Like, I think you write the best mysteries. And I would like to be a writer like you. And my father is in the Amazon, and he sent me this medicine stick. And I thought I could maybe write a story about it and magic and stuff — and here, and . . . ."

"Hold on a second, old man. Have to write something down." Thomas whirled around, grabbed a pencil and a notebook from the table where the typewriter stood and scribbled furiously. "A chap has to seize ideas when they come. Mustn't let those rascals escape." He tapped the pencil against his teeth, closed his eyes briefly, then set the pencil on top of the notebook and turned back to Nick. "Now what were you saying?"

Talking to Thomas Turner wasn't so frightening after all. He didn't seem to be paying much attention. Nick spoke clearly and carefully. "I wondered if you'd come over Saturday afternoon, for a cup of tea."

"By jove. Jolly decent of you. Saturday? Saturday?" Thomas Turner nodded several times, and then shook his head. "Seems to me there's something about Saturday. Got it! Have to go to a book launch Saturday. That's it. A book launch. That's it, by jove."

"Sunday then?" said Nick.

"Righty ho. Sunday it is. Quite so. Sunday," said Thomas Turner. "Have to write that down."

"I can't find the one you mean," called Nick. He was down on his hands and knees in front of the sideboard, peering into the bottom compartment. "I see the sherry and a full bottle of gin, but no brandy. Wait a minute." He leaned closer and stared into the dark interior. "I can't see what's in the back. Behind this stuff."

"I'm sure there's some left in there. I never use it except when I make dessert crêpes," called his mother from the kitchen.

Nick was glad that his mother had decided that she wanted something special to eat — something as exotic as fresh peach crêpes Suzette. He was determined to find cooking brandy, as long as there was cooking brandy to be found.

He ran to the kitchen, grabbed the flashlight from a shelf near the back door and squatted down in front of the sideboard again. The sherry bottle, front and centre, was the only item that had been moved in the past six months, judging by the look of things. The inner reaches of the cupboard were grey with dust and a small cobweb fluttered in one corner.

He shone the flashlight around an assortment of liqueur bottles, flower vases, bronzed baby shoes, ashtrays and a figurine of a tall thin blue lady holding a basket of flowers. And an almost-full bottle of brandy! There, behind a black vase with enamelled red poppies and green ivy trailing down its sides.

"Got it!" he called.

"Good. Thank you, Nick," said his mother in her Loving Mother Price voice.

Nick tried to tell himself that everything was all right now as he walked into his bedroom. He stopped dead in his tracks. Why wasn't the face on the medicine stick smiling? He was absolutely sure that he had turned it smiling face out when he carried it in and hung it on the waiting silver hook. Because Allison had asked him to "keep watching the feathers, Nick. You know. Just when you think of it. Watch to see if they seem to point anywhere."

The feathers did not seem to point anywhere. They drooped over the stone face. He stepped closer. The face scowled. A cold sweat formed between his shoulder blades. Who could have turned it around? He lunged toward the stick, hand outstretched to grab it. It smiled. Impossible. He stepped back. It scowled. He stepped forward. It smiled.

Aw, just the shadows changing. Don't be a boob, Nick.

But maybe it was trying to tell him something. That was it! When he backed off, it scowled. When he moved ahead, it smiled. That meant move ahead. Don't back off. But move ahead where? How?

He lay down on his bed to think. The medicine stick looked down on him, seeming to nod in approval. Something nagged at the edge of his mind. Something he had seen, or heard, or smelled during the day wasn't quite right.

He got out his list and read it. *Car moved on ferry. A strangled and stabbed scarecrow. Bulldozer damaged. Hall burned down. Photograph gouged. Phone call. Threatening message sprayed on with shaving cream. A medicine stick and his mother's illness.* What did they all have in common? Brazil? The Amazon rainforests? The phone call definitely sounded like jungle music and tropical birds in the background. Fires in the jungle. Fires here on the island. SAVE THE ISLAND FOREST! SAVE THE RAINFOREST! Developers and loggers with fierce angry feelings. Red fish scales, red ibises, red tassels on llamas, red scarf, red fires. Pink dolphins. Silver shirt labels. A grey shirt label. Birds that sound like running water. Something thrown into the water. Howling monkeys, barking dogs. Foghorns. Giant waves. Cows jumping off rafts. Stink bugs. Smelly otter droppings. Water purified with chlorine. What would Dad do about this? I wonder what he's doing now? Eating more potatoes? Slapping at mosquitoes? Purifying water? All of the above? Nick closed his eyes and imagined his father, wearing his new Bell shirt, his black hair falling over his forehead as he carefully poured chlorine bleach powder into a canteen. No. They don't use chlorine anymore. They use . . . . His eyes flew open and he sat up.

Powder! That was it. Something to do with powder. White. White powder where no white powder should be. He leaned forward with his elbows on his bent knees and his chin in his hands and closed his eyes again.

A light went on inside Nick's head. Crêpes Suzette! Cooking brandy! A half-full bottle of sherry, and beside it, picked up by the flashlight's beam, faint circles where there was no dust. One circle outlined with dust, but lighter dust. White dust. That was it! White dust around where his mother's sherry bottle had been standing. Flu. Had the flu come and gone with the sherry? Was sherry causing the so-called flu? Nick's heart pounded and thoughts shot around in his head like a laser show.

He jumped up and rushed into the living room, snatching up the flashlight as he ran.

"What's up, Nick?" His mother raised her head from the steaming griddle.

Nick's heart was pounding and his breath came in short gasps as he held the flashlight at floor level and examined the white powder on the cabinet floor.

"Mom," he called. "Come here." His voice rose with excitement and fear as he talked.

"Just a sec, Nick. I have to turn the crêpes," she called from the kitchen.

"Well, hurry," he said.

In a split second she was standing beside him, a spatula in one hand. "What is it?"

"See?" He held the flashlight close to the powdery area and pointed. His finger shook. "It must be something put in your sherry. Not the flu. When you feel better you drink it. Then you get sick again. Maybe it's poison. Can we get it tested? Call the police. Don't drink any of it! You won't, will you?" He looked at her anxiously.

She was staring at him as though she had never seen him before. "What are you talking about, Nick?"

"Look. Right there. See? It's powder of some kind. Around your sherry bottle."

"But how is that possible?" She knelt beside him and stared into the cabinet, then she swallowed and placed the back of her hand against her forehead. The spatula looked like some kind of hair decoration she was trying on. Pretty funny, but Nick didn't feel like laughing.

She spoke slowly and her voice was low. "It's possible,

I suppose. Something could be in the sherry. But who? And why?"

"You won't drink it, will you, Mom? You won't, will you?" Nick stared into her face.

"No, Nick. I won't drink it." She put a hand on his shoulder, shook her head and frowned.

"Jonathan said his magazine was moved. I guess maybe he was right. It did get moved and wrinkled when somebody . . . ." The telephone rang and Nick sat back and tried to remember exactly when his mother had been sick. Had it always been after drinking the sherry?

He heard her puzzled voice. "No. She left here around four o'clock."

Nick held his breath, waiting for the next words.

"I don't think so. Wait a minute and I'll ask Nick." She turned from the telephone. "Nick, did Allison intend to go anywhere, after she left here?"

"No," said Nick slowly. He couldn't explain about Max.

"No. Probably nothing to worry about," said Patricia into the telephone. "That's right. Maybe she stopped to have a quick swim. Or met somebody she knew and decided to have a Coke. Yes, they lose track of time. Well, listen. Nick will hop on his bike and check out the beach and the coffee shop. Won't you, Nick?" She turned to look at him and he nodded.

"Yes. Give us a call when she turns up, won't you?"

Nick jumped on his bike and pedalled up the driveway as fast as he could go. There was a cloud of smoke hanging over the road. Uncle Haylett must have a pretty big fire going in his wood stove. Black smoke, too. Looked kind of dangerous. Fluffy bits of soot floated around. Thomas Turner was walking along Decourcey Drive with his head bent, shoulders slouched and his hands, holding a book, clasped behind his back.

Oh, no. Here come Beaver and Grolinski! Nick swallowed

hard and pedalled faster. He yelled "Yo" as he passed his friends, and careened around the bend toward the beach.

He threw his bike onto the grass and raced across the baseball diamond to the beach at Taylor Bay. People were barbecuing and having picnics. He hurried up and down the beach, searching for Allison.

He could see the heads of three swimmers some distance from shore, but there was no way of telling who they were. He raced around the edge of the baseball diamond, among the picnic tables, along the bush-enclosed path from the roadway and under the tall trees, looking for her bicycle.

"Hi, Nick. You looking for somebody? How's your mother? Hey there, Nick. What's the hurry?" The voice came from a young woman who was holding a baby, one of Nick's mother's friends.

Nick wasn't sure why he didn't want to tell anybody about Allison. He was afraid. That was it. Afraid that if he said her name out loud his voice would break and his eyes would fill with tears.

"No. Just a towel. Jonathan lost one," he yelled.

"Does it have penguins on it?" called a woman, pointing behind a pile of logs.

Nick shook his head. "No. Thanks. I don't see it." His voice was hoarse.

Back on the road, he pedalled like fury. He brought his bike to a skidding stop in the parking lot in front of the shopping complex. A quick glance up and down the four aisles in the store revealed no sign of Allison. Maybe she was at the back where the greeting cards and videos were kept.

A large woman was bending over a child beside the book display. "You must choose the one you want, Melanie." There was no way around her.

Nick wheeled and rushed down the next aisle. An old man was looking at cabbages.

"Just a small one, Rafe," said a white-haired stooped old woman. "Mind what I say. You know well as I do you're not over-fond of cabbage."

Why is everybody in the whole world trying to get in my way?

Nick rode around the outside of the shopping complex, past the liquor store, the Island Crafts Shoppe, the hairdressers', the hardware store. No red bicycle. No girl with long hair and blue eyes. And forget-me-nots on the pocket of her shirt. It was the forget-me-nots that seemed to be causing the lump in his throat.

No red bicycle or blue-eyed girl at the Island Steak 'n' Pizza.

Nick jammed on his brakes at Max's driveway. A flock of starlings bent their knees backward, jumped from the fence straight up into the air and flew off in a dark cloud.

Nobody was at home at Max's house. Not even the dog. Nick scrambled his way past the old cars and parts of old cars around to the back yard.

There ain't nobody here but us chickens. *Geez! Why did that nonsense pop into my head? Because there ain't. Nobody home. But the chickens.*

The clothesline had been fixed, but the only thing hanging from it was a faded pink J-cloth. He held his hands at the sides of his face and looked in every window except the two in the attic under the gable roof.

"Allison," he called softly.

"Allison?" Louder.

The house was silent and still.

He heard a car engine and ran back to his bicycle. The car did not slow down. It went past with a roar.

Allison must be home by now, he thought. She probably stopped to pick blackberries. Took the long way around Decourcey Drive, because the blackberries are thickest on the far side, and he just missed seeing her. She was sitting at the supper table with her family at that very minute.

Allison was not at home. Nick knew it the instant he turned the corner at the Twin Beaches sign and saw her parents and two of the loggers standing near the Taylor Bay Cottages. Nick's heart turned to lead.

"Mr. McKeghnie?" Nick spoke to Allison's father.

"Yeah?" He clapped his left hand to his forehead and closed his eyes. "Yeah?" Mr. McKeghnie turned to look at Nick.

"Allison was at our place . . . ."

"Oh, yeah. Right. She didn't say anything? About going some place else?" The man stared into Nick's eyes as though willing him to remember something that would help.

Nick shook his head numbly.

"Did anybody phone the police?" said one of the loggers. "They should be watching at the ferry, especially for vans. A guy can be carrying anything in one of those things."

"I did." It was Allison's mother. She was biting her lower lip and her hands were clenched at her sides. "They said they couldn't do anything. She hasn't been missing for twenty-four hours."

Nick's blood froze. The horrible unnamed fear in his head took shape. Maybe somebody did abduct her. Stopped to ask directions and then held a gun to her head and forced her to get into a van, and . . . .

His stomach rose and he felt like throwing up.

"We gotta do something," said the logger. "Start rounding up the neighbours, many as we can." He was off on the run.

Nick jumped on his bicycle and pedalled frantically toward home. He would hunt for Allison by himself. He would scour every inch . . . . Maybe if he really concentrated, really, really concentrated as hard as he could, he'd think of something. Some clue. Some small sign.

Go home. Start from there. Think! Think! Think! Can't think. Brain in overdrive. Hands shake. Horrible taste in mouth.

Nobody was home at the Prices', but Nick didn't take time to wonder why. He raced into his bedroom.

The list! Where's the list? Read it again. And again. Words don't make sense. Look like chicken scratches. Chickens. Max's chickens. Feathers. Red feathers. White feathers. Ibis feathers. Eagle feathers. A feather in a book. Feathers on a medicine stick. Medicine stick feathers? Medicine stick feathers! Allison would ask the medicine stick for help. There was a small grain of comfort in thinking about what Allison would do. And what she would say. *"We have to believe we can solve it, Nick." I will believe. I will believe, Allison!*

He reached for the medicine stick and lifted it from the silver hook. It seemed to welcome him and it felt warm and alive in his hands.

Stand in the middle of the room. Go into a trance.

He clutched the stick to his chest with both hands and slowly moved his lowered head from side to side so that the feathers brushed his cheeks and lips and chin.

"Help me. Help me find her. Please. Help . . . me . . . find . . . her." He whispered to the feathered stick and then moved his hands so that he was clutching it with the right hand above the left, as Allison had instructed. But her hands should be in between his. Her hands. He could almost feel them pressing his. He *could* feel her hands.

"Where is she?" Nick felt himself become still. Absolutely still. And calm. His heartbeat slowed down. His breathing became soft and even. His brain did not think. He felt calm and powerful at the same time. Then pictures started to form before his half-closed eyes.

He and Allison were crouched in the forest, listening. They could hear the sound of a bulldozer crashing over the cliff.

The scene changed. Allison was opening a book, *Terror on the Island.* A feather floated out from between the pages.

The scene changed again. He was alone. He watched

himself answer a telephone. It was the middle of the night. "Hello? Hello?" A muffled rasping voice. "Tell her to leave the island." And in the background, other sounds. The garbled sounds of a so-called "talking" bird.

He jerked his head up suddenly. A feather he had seen. A sound he had heard. He knew. In one explosion of thought he knew. He knew where Allison was. And he knew who had taken her there.

"Thank you," he breathed to the medicine stick with one gigantic breath as he laid it on the bed and raced for the back door.

Chapter 20

It wouldn't start! The bloody thing wouldn't start. Nick knelt in the small boat as it bobbed near the shore in front of the house. Again and again he wound the rope around the starter pulley and yanked. A sickening *rrr-rrr-rrr*. Again, *rrr-rrr-rrr*. And again. And again.

He hadn't used the dinghy lately. He preferred the kayak now. Poke the knot over the groove. Wind the rope fast. Yank! *Brr-rrr-putt — gasp-putt-gasp-putt-putt-putt*. At last the motor coughed into life and he pulled the throttle open wide. He waited, kneeling over the motor, adjusting levers, until it had settled into a steady humming rhythm.

Nick grabbed up an oar and used it to push against the sandy bottom to get into deeper water, then locked the motor in place and pulled the lever to the forward position. The boat took off with a roar. Now that he was actually on his way, he was not at all sure that the encounter with the medicine stick had been anything but a creation of his own crazy imagination. Still, it was the only chance he knew of. Worth a try.

At this speed it wouldn't take long. The water was calm. The dinghy's bow rose into the air and the small boat planed toward the entrance to the bay. The spray on Nick's face felt cool and soothing. He kept one hand firmly on the steering and throttle stick. His eyes scanned the water ahead. All he needed was to hit a floating log or a deadhead now. He must be extra careful. Extra alert.

The motor coughed. The boat lurched. Nick's heart lurched. Please. Please. Don't stop. Don't stop. Don't stop. DON'T STOP! Nick pulled frantically at the choke lever. The motor stopped. The boat bobbed around like a useless speck of driftwood on the wide ocean. Nick swallowed the lump in his throat and blinked back tears.

His arms ached and his lungs were bursting by the time he rowed back to shore and hoisted the dinghy up onto the rocks. He'd have to take his kayak. But he couldn't. He wouldn't have room for Allison. Unless she could ride on the back like he'd taught her to do. If she was there. But what if she fell off in deep water, and was too nervous to get back on without tipping the kayak? He'd have to take the two-seater. It would be slower, but . . . .

He ripped the tarpaulin off the big kayak, half expecting to see his father's tall frame hunched in the front seat, and hear his voice singing "Paddlin' Madeline Home." He knew that if Jim Price could see him now — getting out the big kayak for the first time in two years, he would be nodding at him and saying, "Atta boy, Nick."

Dip-splash, splash-splash-splash. Nick sat in the back seat and pulled with the double-sided paddle harder than he had ever pulled in his life. The kayak skimmed along, looking very long and very empty in front of his straining eyes.

Although the sea was calm, there was a surging swell. The first one caught him by surprise. He had been so busy looking for the tide level on the high bank beside him that he hadn't noticed the big ferry heading past Entrance Light toward Departure Bay. The swell hit the kayak sideways. It turned on its side and Nick leaned in the other direction as hard as he could.

He was close to the rocks. One more big swell could smash him into them. He watched now as the swells approached and turned to face into each one, paddling desperately to make some headway along the steep cliffs between each surge. The double kayak was much harder to control than the smaller one. His arms were numb and his throat felt dry and sore as he gasped for breath. He manoeuvred around an outcropping of rock.

The rock should be sticking up higher in the water.

The tide is halfway in!

He glanced at his watch. It couldn't be 8 o'clock. High tide yesterday was at 8:15 PM. Add one hour, more or less, and that would make it 9:15 today. He had, maybe, twenty minutes to reach Allison.

It's going to be too late. Gotta go back. Get somebody with a fast boat.

But there was no time to go back. Nick wished he could remember what level it would reach today. Would it be a high high, or a low high? Not that it would matter. The lowest high would be too high for Allison. If she was there.

He thought about her long blond hair floating under the sea, entangled with seaweed. Her blue eyes, staring and cold. As lifeless as the scarecrow's old brown pine cone eyes. He paddled harder.

He rounded a sharp promontory of jagged rock and slipped into Connery Cove. The high cliffs surrounding the beach were alive with cormorants. They perched on outcroppings and roots and held their wings out to dry. Usually Nick liked to watch the community of black birds moving in and out of the cliffside — making it seem alive with their movements. He didn't glance up today. He kept his eyes riveted on the area just above the water line. There was only about eighteen inches of dry land between the lapping water and the base of the perpendicular cliff.

No Allison.

He jumped into the water and threw the yellow nylon rope attached to the ring at the bow of the kayak over a boulder. His eyes darted around. He turned to make sure the kayak was securely fastened and caught a glimpse of something white floating near the rocks on the other side of the cove.

Allison's shoe. Both shoes. He could see the other one now, bumping up and down on the sand as the waves lifted it.

So she must be here. Somewhere. Behind one of the

big boulders. Or did she try to swim for it? Impossibly far for anybody but a marathon swimmer. So many barnacle-covered sharp rocks to skirt. And the cliff, jutting up from hundreds of feet below the water all along this piece of coastline, except for the small cove where he was standing.

Thank God! She hadn't tried to swim for it. She was lying on her side, on a small patch of sand between two boulders. She looked as though she was wedged into place, like driftwood tossed into a crevice by the tide. Her knees were drawn up, her head bowed down, her arms clutched around her shoulders. In her right hand, she held an almost-empty plastic 7-Up bottle. Nick's knees turned to mush and buckled under him. Was she dead?

He crawled closer and touched her arm.

"Allison?"

She didn't move.

He grabbed her wrist and tried to pull her hand away from her shoulder, but it was frozen in place.

Don't dead people's bodies get limp?

Nick swallowed and pulled harder. Allison's head moved. Her eyes opened, then closed again. She mumbled something.

Energy poured into Nick's body like a rushing torrent. She was alive! Allison was alive! Nothing else mattered. He felt as strong as Samson. He could pick her up and carry her over boulders, over mountains, if necessary. He had got there in time. Allison was alive.

Allison was trying to say something. He leaned closer. "What?" he said.

"Who are you? . . . dream . . . angels . . . ." She mumbled and dropped her head back down against her chest.

"Allison! Come on! It's me. We gotta get out of here." Nick scrambled around, knelt beside her and tried to get his arm around her waist.

Allison opened her eyes again, blinked and slowly sat up, reaching for the rock edge with one hand. The other

one still clutched the plastic bottle. Her face was swollen
with wasp stings and her hair was matted and snarled.
Nick recognized the red welts spreading from the deep
scratches on her feet — barnacle scrapes.

"It . . . is . . . you." She seemed to be having trouble trying to make her lips say the words. "It's really you. Oh,
Nicholas." Tears filled her eyes. She raised herself to her
knees, put both arms around his neck and clung to him.

"It's okay." He patted her back and brushed sand from
her hair. "You're okay. I've got the big kayak. We'll get out
of here." Her grip on his shoulders slackened and she sank
back down in a heap.

"Too late. Too . . . tired," she sobbed and hiccuped
against her forearm.

"No. It's not too late. Can you walk? Come on. I can
help you."

"No, Nick. Don't . . . think I can. Tired."

Nick tried to pull her up, but her body was limp and
heavy.

She started to shiver. "I'm cold," she whispered as she
raised a trembling hand up to him.

She's cold? She's cold? How can she be cold?

Thoughts raced around Nick's head. She was acting
funny. Like his mom when she had the flu, only more so.
Her eyes were not focusing properly and her muscles
didn't seem to be working. The medicine stick spell? No.
Probably more white powder!

"What's that? What's in there?" He tried to take the
bottle from her, but her hand wouldn't release it.

"Huh?" Allison's forehead was wrinkled and her eyes
were narrowed as though she were trying very hard to
concentrate. She shivered.

*Why is she cold? On a warm day. It's shock. She's in shock.
That's why she's cold.*

He fumbled with the buttons of his shirt, and then
ripped it off, sending two buttons popping into the water,

which was now lapping at his feet. He wrapped the shirt around Allison, put both of his arms around her waist and tried to pull her up.

Allison managed to get shakily to her feet. There was perspiration on her forehead and her face was white, except for the red welts on her lips and cheekbones where the wasps had stung her. The front of her shirt was splattered with water and her hair was stringy from seawater and spittle. Her eyes were swollen and red.

"Nick!" She seemed surprised, as though she had just recognized him. She smiled a small weak smile, and he thought she had never looked more beautiful. She started to shiver again.

He helped her put one arm into his shirtsleeve, then persuaded her to transfer the bottle to her left hand while he helped her with the other sleeve. She was quite obviously not going to part with that crazy bottle. Getting it away from her would be like trying to take Jonathan's pacifier away from him when he was a baby. Nick buttoned the four remaining buttons over the blue forget-me-nots.

"Got to do it. Got to make it to the kayak. See," He pointed with one hand. "Just that far. Come on. We can do it."

He tried to lift her and support her weight while she walked, but her body was too limp and heavy. There was only one way. He had to carry her.

"Allison, I'm going to piggy-back you. When I bend over, you lean on my back."

But she couldn't hold on. When he tried to stand straight, holding her legs at his sides, she slipped down and splashed like a rag doll in the shallow water.

"Okay. Allison!" he yelled at her. "Concentrate! Remember riding the kayak. Concentrate like that. I'm going to hoist you over my shoulder." Nick was not at all sure that he *could* hoist her over his shoulder, but he called on the power of the medicine stick. "Just this one last wish, please," he whispered. "Just let us make it to the kayak and I'll never ask for magic again."

He did get her over his shoulder. And with a grunt and a heave he managed to stand erect.

Allison was muttering something. Her head was dangling near his knees, and he had both arms up around her back as he stumbled around trying to get his balance. "What?"

"Sack of spuds." Was she trying to make a joke? She was. She was actually trying to make a joke. Her head and arms were dangling limply in front of Nick. Her legs and hips were bumping against him from behind, dripping water down the back of his leg. And she was giggling.

"Yeah. Sack of spuds. Weighs a ton!" Nick gasped. He staggered around and then took one small step. He could make it to the pile of driftwood, he was pretty sure of that. He shuffled his feet along in the water, taking short steps. He tested for footing before putting his weight on each leg. But how the heck was he going to get her over the driftwood?

He had to let her down on the big logs, push and nudge her over the uneven mounds and pick her up again on the other side. But she seemed to be getting a little more sensible. She was able to help herself. By the time they were over the pile, into water up to their knees, she said she thought she could walk, with his help. They splashed and stumbled their way to the kayak.

Now how could he get her in? How do you get a limp body into a bobbing kayak? "With a great deal of — " gasp "— difficulty," said Nick as he tried to steady the boat with one hand and help her with the other.

"Pardon?" said Allison. She stopped moving and looked at him.

"What happens when a resistible force meets a movable object?" Nick smiled at her. "How are *we* going to get *you* in there?" He pointed to the front seat. "Easier if we could ground it first." He looked around. Not much chance of grounding the kayak. But maybe if he held it against a big log it would help steady the hull.

It did, and Allison finally did manage with Nick's help to lift one leg high enough to get it into the right place. Then he gave a lift and a shove with both arms around her waist and the kayak bobbed and danced around, but Allison was in, except for her right leg. She was still holding the bottle.

Nick was in waist-high water now. But Allison was in the kayak, and it was a piece of cake from now on. Should he tie her in? If they hit a bad swell and it tipped sideways, could she fall out? But if it tipped right over and she was tied in? That would be worse. She couldn't possibly swim in this state. Better just concentrate very hard on keeping the kayak nice and steady in the water.

He pulled a life vest out from under the bow, tied it on her, jumped in and started home. His arms weren't behaving very well; the muscles were sore and trembling. But the water was as smooth as silk now. No wash from ferries or freighters or cruisers to contend with. Allison was right there, in front of him, and her voice was getting stronger.

"You okay, Allison?"

"Yes, Nick. Are you?" She turned her head to answer.

"Fine. Fine. Can't seem to paddle very fast, but . . . ."

"That's okay." She gave a small wave of her hand over her shoulder. "Do it your way. You know best. Your mom is right, you know?"

"How's that?" he said.

"You really are one of the good guys, Nick. You really are."

As they turned into Taylor Bay, Nick even had enough energy left to sing some snatches of his dad's song. Only the words were a little different: "Paddlin' Allison Home."

Chapter 21

By the time they reached the little bay in front of Nick's house, Allison was feeling so much better that she wanted to help pull the kayak out of the water.

"No." Nick jumped out on a flat rock and gave her his hand. "We'll leave it here for now. I'll get it later." He helped her step onto the rock, then played out the bow rope so the boat was bobbing several feet from shore and tied it to a tree trunk.

"We gotta call your folks right away."

But it was Patricia Price who made the call. "Didn't you see the note I left you?" she asked, when Nick wanted to know where she'd been.

Nick shook his head.

"Right here by the telephone." She picked up a scrap of paper and read aloud: "Phone lines all busy. Gone to talk to Pickerings about Allison. One of the kids might have seen her."

A few minutes later Allison's father burst in on the run, not waiting to knock. He gathered Allison up into his arms, then shook Nick's hand and called him a hero.

Allison's mother and sisters were not far behind. Her mother cried and then laughed and then did both at the same time and kissed her daughter's forehead and hugged Nick.

The doctor came and examined Allison, congratulated Nick for his resourcefulness and told Allison's mother to call him immediately if her temperature fluctuated. He took the plastic bottle to be analyzed.

Jonathan would not stop asking questions. "Uncle Hayloft? How come Uncle Hayloft made Allison go to

Connery Cove? And left her there to get drownded?"

"We don't know why, Jonathan. We just know he did," his mother replied.

"Why did he leave that drink for you? Was it poison?" Jonathan had crouched down beside the couch to look into Allison's face. "If you were already going to get drownded? How could he kill you twice?"

"It wasn't poison. The doctor thinks it was some kind of narcotic. To make me sleepy and mixed-up." Allison cupped her hand around his cheek, looked past him at Nick and smiled.

There was a knock at the door, and Constable Mike Carruthers walked into the Prices' living room. "I expect our man will be back soon. His boat is gone, so he can't be out much longer. It's getting pretty late." He sank into a chair and held out his hand for the cup of coffee Nick's mother was offering. "I thought it best to wait until he gets in the house and then confront him," he added. "Larry's got the place staked out. He'll give us a shout on the pager, soon as anybody arrives."

"Do you take anything in it?" Patricia asked.

"A little milk, if you don't mind." Constable Carruthers laid his hat on the coffee table and leaned back.

Nick was sitting on the floor in a strategic position for Allison-watching.

Allison was lying on the couch, propped up with pillows. Her mother was sitting in a chair beside her, feeling her forehead from time to time with the palm of her hand. Her father was standing in front of the sliding patio doors, holding his right arm — in its heavy cast — with his left one.

"You the young fellow who found her?" The policeman looked at Nick.

"Yeah," said Nick.

"Good work!" He nodded his thanks as Patricia poured milk into his coffee cup.

"Good work is right," said Allison's father. He carefully picked up a mug of steaming coffee from the dining table and moved toward an armchair.

"Jonathan, I'd like you to pass the muffins, please," said his mother. Jonathan didn't seem to hear. He was trying to impress Allison's youngest sister, Stephanie, with the extent of his knowledge about *Mad* magazine linguistics. They were lying side by side on the floor, stomach down, under a trilight.

"I'll pass the muffins, Mrs. Price," said ten-year-old Jane, the other McKeghnie sister. "If you like."

"Thank you, Jane," said Patricia with a smile.

It was almost 11:30, way past bedtime for at least three of the gathered company, but nobody could think of sleep until a criminal had been caught.

The trip back from Connery Cove in the two-person kayak, with Allison's lumpy life jacket-encased figure in front of him, now seemed to Nick as unreal as the medicine stick's magic. Something he had imagined.

How could Uncle Haylett do that? Not really an uncle, but a relative. They had always thought of him as an uncle, he and Jonathan. And treated him like an uncle. They invited him over for Christmas and Thanksgiving. They made valentines for him and fed his animals when he was away for a couple of days. How could he do that? Force Allison to get into his old truck and then into his battered old boat, leaving her at Connery Cove. He told her he would come back for her, but he would have been too late.

What if the medicine stick hadn't made me think of Connery Cove? wondered Nick. He felt panic start to rise inside him at the thought. He remembered the bird in the phone call saying "grok, greek, glk." Only he kept thinking of ibises, because of the music in the background, instead of Uncle Haylett's bird. And the bulldozer roaring away in Connery Cove. The bird and the bulldozer. What if he hadn't got there in time? His skin crawled. He shivered and quickly pushed the thoughts away.

Excited and relieved voices flowed around Nick, ask-

ing questions, exclaiming about his bravery, marvelling at
his common sense. He felt as though he were being given
a great deal more credit than he really deserved.

Now they were just waiting. Waiting for Uncle Haylett
to arrive home and be arrested. The two policemen would
knock at the door and tell him he was being charged with
kidnapping. Allison and Nick would wait outside in the
police car with Allison's father, available if they were
needed to confront the man.

"I'm starving," said Allison.

Three people jumped up.

"What would you like, Allison. Toast?" said Nick's mother.

"Want another muffin?" said Jane.

"I'll get it," said Nick. "A glass of milk? A grilled
cheese?" He moved closer and looked into her eyes. She
looked steadily back at him and winked one wasp-stung
eyelid. Nick smiled broadly, his stomach did a funny flip-
flop and he felt a wonderful warm glow spreading through
him. He and Allison shared something that nobody else in
the world could totally understand. Only the two of them
would ever know what it had really been like — at Connery Cove with the seagulls crying overhead and the waves
lapping over their feet and ankles. He winked back.

The beeper on the policeman's pager sounded. All
heads turned as Constable Mike Carruthers held the in-
strument near his mouth and spoke into it. "He's just getting
out of the truck?" he asked. "He's unlocking the door?" He
listened, his face solemn and still, then said, "Yeah, okay.
We'll drive right past and park close in to the bush there."
He listened intently. "No. I don't think we better take a
chance, pulling into the driveway. You never know what
he might have up his sleeve . . . . Okay. Sure . . . . These kids
have had enough scares for one day. Yeah. Don't want to
take a chance. Come on. He's home." He stood and looked
at Allison and Nick and started toward the door.

Chapter 22

Nick and Allison sat in the back seat of the police car.
Mr. McKeghnie was in the front seat, with instructions
about which button to push after they heard the words,
"Come in now," on the radio receiver.

Mr. McKeghnie's broad shoulders, outlined against the
car windshield, looked solid and comforting. Nick rolled
down the window and listened to the sounds of the night
birds and the sigh of the outgoing tide. A car door
slammed in the distance and laughing muted voices sang
something about an island called home.

Allison sighed a ragged uneven sigh and Nick reached
for her hand. "It's okay. Don't be scared," he said.

"Are you all right, Allison?" Her father turned so his
square-chinned profile was silhouetted in the faint light
from the radio instruments.

"Yeah. I'm okay, Dad," said Allison.

The radio receiver crackled. "Come in now," said a
voice.

Allison's father helped her out of the car and held her
hand as they waited for Nick. She reached for his hand
with her free one and they walked toward the lighted window. She stumbled.

"This is too much for you, Allison." Her father stopped
and looked at her. "You don't have to do this. I'll go in and
tell them. You go back to the car with Nick."

"No." Allison shook her head. "I'm going. He can't
hurt me with two policemen and you and Nick there." Although Nick was anxious and tense, hearing Allison put
him in the same category as two RCMP constables and her
own father made him feel proud. He squeezed her hand

and she clung to his even tighter.

They could hear Haylett Croft's loud and angry voice as they approached the house. "You guys are nuts. They always send the losers to the Islands. Out of your minds. What earthly reason could I have . . . ?" He stopped speaking and his jaw dropped open as Allison stepped through the doorway.

Haylett was sitting on a kitchen chair wearing handcuffs. His grouchy grey cat was crouched on the end of the wood-burning stove, looking as though it were about to pounce. The budgie was screeching from its cage beside the bright green and yellow couch.

Nick had a faint sense of something familiar but unusual in the room, but he didn't have time to think about it now. His head was spinning. Surely this was not Uncle Haylett. This man who was jerking his head from side to side, opening and closing his mouth like a fish, kicking first one and then the other foot and stomping them down on the linoleum floor. A wave of sadness swept over Nick.

"You!" Haylett spat the word at Allison. "Meddling brassy young creature. See what your interfering ways got you?" He lunged toward her, his manacled wrists outstretched.

"Steady there, Mr. Croft." The two policemen each had a hand on one of his shoulders and pulled him back into the chair.

He sat with a thump. His grey bushy hair was sticking out in all directions and his small square glasses slid down his nose. He reached up with one hand to push them back into place and the handcuffs jerked against his other wrist.

"Bloody brat! You don't even belong on this island. Come where you're not wanted. And get your nose into other people's business. It's all your fault." He continued to harangue Allison. "I didn't want to hurt you." He shook his head angrily. "I didn't want to hurt anybody. I just wanted what rightly belongs to me. All my life other people been taking advantage. I do all the work, they get all the credit. I save my money and try to get ahead, they skin me out of it. You got no business having that place." He looked angrily at Nick now. "That property belongs to me by rights."

"What property?" Nick was taken aback.

"That place you're living in. That belongs to me by rights," he snarled.

"But Great-Grandfather left it to my dad in his will," said Nick.

"Yeah. Bloody old fool. Your dad cozied up to the old codger, that's why. Besides, it was left to your father as long as he lives there and uses it. He's not living in it now, is he? Is he?" He lunged toward Nick.

Nick shook his head.

"So it should be mine. Should have been mine in the first place. I'm the oldest son of the oldest son. Your father isn't even the son of a son. He's the son of a daughter. Don't know what got into the old coot. Something rotten in Denmark."

"But my dad looked after Granddad when he was sick." Nick was angry now at the suggestion that his father had taken unfair advantage of an old man. "I remember, my dad and mother worried a lot about him. He lived with us for quite a while, and then Dad visited him every single day when he was in the hospital. You never helped then."

"Nah! Your sweet loving parents poisoned the old man's mind against me. I should have that land, especially now. Your dad not even living on it. Just his wife and two brats." Uncle Haylett shook his head and tears stood in his eyes. For a moment Nick felt sorry for him — until he remembered Allison's shivering face and frightened eyes at Connery Cove.

"Too bad you had to get too smart for your own good," said Haylett, looking at Allison. "I heard you and Nick talking about gasoline and snooping around. I sneaked around through Turner's place and watched from over there, when you came with that letter. You thought I wasn't around, but I saw you pick up that old rag in the carport, the one I use for wiping up oil and stuff. Piece of an old shirt. You smelled it. Then you stared at the gasoline can and I knew you had it figured out.

"All I needed was a little time. Get you out of the way. Burn up those other old shirts used to belong to Jim, get rid of the gasoline can — anything that might look bad for me. Still had the shaving cream tin hidden in the back yard, too. Hadn't been able to figure out how to get rid of it. People is so hell-bent on keeping track of any kind of stuff gets thrown in the ocean. So had to get you out of the way, that's all, just out of the way." Haylett slumped down in the chair and lowered his voice.

"Wasn't going to leave you there. Told you I'd be back. I didn't mean to harm a hair on your head. You got nothing to do with it. Nothing at all to do with it. But you brought it all on yourself. Too big for your britches. Nosing around other people's business. I didn't want anybody to get hurt. That's what I wanted most of all. For nobody to get hurt. I tried going back, too. I did. 'Cause it would be just your word against mine, then. Knew you'd have to drink it. The water. Knew you would. And you'd be hallucinating. Nobody would believe you, but — " He sat bolt upright, his face became rigid and set, and his eyes blazed.

"I want what's rightly mine. My dad told me from the time I was a tad that the place would be mine someday. And it is. It really is mine. People cheated me out of what was rightly mine. And so I had no choice, did I now? Just had to take it into my own hands. Get Jim's family off the place and it would belong to me. How do you think it feels? Sitting here in this little shack on this dirty little roadside, looking across there at a place right on the waterfront — valuable — as pretty a spot as you'd find anywhere, and other people having it. When it's rightly mine." He shook his head angrily.

"Ark. Yawk. Grok, crok." The grey budgie was hopping up and down in its cage yelling at the top of its lungs.

"But why did you do all those other things?" said Constable Brown. "They had nothing to do with waterfront property. Why burn down the hall and send that bulldozer crashing over the cliff and string wire in the trees where the loggers were going?"

"Stir things up a bit. Get people riled. Patricia was right in the middle of that tomfoolery. I figured the more hard feelings were going on around the island, the more likely she'd get scared away. And then I was ready to jump right in and claim what's mine. The lawyers told me soon as the place was vacated it could probably be mine. I'm the only heir, besides Jim."

"But didn't you get money from Great-Granddad's estate?" asked Nick.

"Money! Money! Sure I got a little money, but what's money compared to land? Land's the only thing that really counts. I want my land!" He lunged from the chair and made a dash for the door.

"Steady as she goes, there," said Constable Carruthers as he grabbed him from behind. "Calm down, now. You'll be coming with us to the police station."

"Yawk, yawk," screeched the bird. "Cree, cree, cree, greedy gree."

"Nick, can you find somebody to tend the animals? Until we get this business sorted out?" said the policeman.

"Sure," said Nick. "Uncle Haylett?" He moved to stand in front of him and looked into his face. "Should I take the dog and the cat and the bird to our place for a while? To look after them?"

"Don't touch one of my animals, you thieving little brat," snarled Haylett. He took a deep breath and his shoulders sagged.

"Just see that they get fed for a day or two, then, will you?" said Mike. Nick nodded. The two policemen took Haylett Croft away.

Before they closed the door Nick had time to look

around and think about what it was that seemed familiar, yet out of place, in Uncle Haylett's house.

That was it! Uncle Haylett did not read popular fiction. "Waste of time, reading that trash," he often said. But a new-looking copy of Thomas Turner's book *Terror on the Island* lay on the arm of the green and yellow couch. Uncle Haylett got his ideas from the book.

"I did go back for you. I did go back. You wasn't there!" Haylett shouted as he climbed into the police car.

The squawking bird's voice grew faint as Nick and Allison and Mr. McKeghnie walked along the road toward the Prices' driveway. The moon was so bright that they could see their shadows.

"Do you feel like talking about it again, Allison?" asked Nick. "Like, I've been wondering how he got you into his truck. But if you don't feel like talking about it, it's okay."

"It's okay," she nodded. "I was snooping around a bit, to be perfectly honest. Trying to get the lid off his garbage can. I didn't hear anything, and then suddenly there was a hand over my mouth and a rope around my arms. I screamed for a second or two when he took his hand away to stuff something in my mouth — some kind of cloth or something, and I tried to fight, hard as I could, but he got me tied up and gagged." She coughed and clasped her hand to her mouth. She sounded as though she might cry. "And, and, he threw me in that truck, on the floor behind the seat. I almost got loose, but by then we were at a funny little beach where he had this boat, and, he, he . . . made me get in it, and took me to that place, that huge cliff, and left me there. That was it. He really didn't mean to hurt me, I believe him on that one. And he did say he would come back. But I was so scared." She jammed her fists hard against her pursed lips.

And she did start to cry.

Chapter 23

Two days later Nick and Allison were sitting on a little patch of sand on a large expanse of flat sandstone. Just a half-mile walk around Decourcey Drive from the Prices' house, and down a twisting public access path, was Nick's and his father's favourite sunset-watching beach. Nick had propped the medicine stick against a twisted tree root which was bleached bare and clean from the movement of the tide and the heat of the sun.

"Allison." Nick turned to face her. "I'm sorry. I got you into that mess with Uncle Haylett. If it hadn't been for me, it never would have happened. I should have known. I shouldn't have let you take that letter by yourself."

"Nick," said Allison softly. "We've been through this before. You saved my life. Sure he said he would come back to get me. And I guess he did try, but it was too late by then. Tell me again. About the medicine stick. How you figured it out."

"I was just holding the stick, trying to concentrate, and I saw this, like a movie in my head." Nick made circular motions with his hands. "The bulldozer crashing over — that meant Connery Cove. And then the feather falling out of the book and the phone call with a bird's screech. It just came to me in a flash, it was Uncle Haylett's bird. It wasn't ibises after all."

"Ibises? Do ibises make sounds?" She tapped his instep with her bare toes and the soft warm feeling rose in Nick.

"I don't know," he laughed. "I thought it must be ibises I heard in that phone call. Because there was jungle music and whistling. But it was a budgie. And a record my dad sent to Uncle Haylett from Brazil. I guess he played it to help disguise his voice. Not very smart of Uncle Haylett, though, forgetting to think about his bird squawking. We owe a lot to that budgie. And the medicine stick."

"So. Do you believe in magic now?" Allison leaned toward him teasingly.

"Well, yeah. Well, no. See . . . ." He laced his fingers together and stared down at them. "I promised I would never ask for any more magic. If it would just help me get you to the kayak. So, I won't. Ask it for anything again. You see?"

"Remember, in the fort? That little piece of feather? It did point in the right direction, didn't it? At your uncle's house. Only we thought it was Thomas Turner's because they live right next door to each other." She cupped her chin in her hands. "It's awesome, if you really think about it. I know everybody says awesome about everything, but this really is awesome, isn't it Nick?"

"Uh-huh. It is. Awesome is right." Nick nodded several times.

"One thing I can't figure out." Allison looked puzzled. "Why did your uncle have shaving cream? He's got a beard."

"Oh. That was Thomas Turner's. He ordered it from town, with eyedrops and stuff. Uncle Haylett brought all the rest of it, and said he forgot the shaving cream. You know — " Nick stared off into the distance "— when I did find out where you were, or thought I did, I should have got help from them, the others. But it seemed so impossible. That you really could be there." He lowered his head and stared at the sand. "And anyway, I thought I had plenty of time." He sighed. "Except the motor quit."

Allison reached for his hand and held it between both of her own.

"You saved my life," she said. "Thank you for saving my life."

"Yeah. If it hadn't been for me your life wouldn't have needed saving in the first place." Nick pulled his hand away. He reached for a stone and threw it into the sea with a swift movement.

"Nicholas." Allison leaned closer. "It wasn't your fault. You were brave and you did all the right things. Even yelling at me." She looked stern.

Allison leaned back against a log and Nick scooped up sand with a seashell, unearthing pieces of beach glass. He piled them in the centre of a yellow float that had detached itself from a fisherman's net and washed ashore.

"Look. Killer whales," Allison gasped.

They stood and shaded their eyes and watched as fountains of water spurted into the air. Great dorsal fins followed by huge black and white bodies surfaced and then disappeared.

"They're beautiful," whispered Allison.

"And smart," said Nick. "Probably just as smart as we are. They just speak a different language and live in a world of water, that's all."

A light breeze rippled the ocean. The red-trimmed white buildings of Entrance Island lighthouse glowed in the setting sun. The sand and rocks and driftwood were warm to the touch. The sky was beginning to turn pink and orange as the sun dropped toward the horizon.

"Holy mackerel, look at all the people out fishing." Nick pointed at two dozen or more small boats circling slowly back and forth around the Five Fingers Islands.

"Nick." Allison shook her head. "Holy mackerel? How corny can you get?" She drew some letters in the sand. A.Y.M.

"What does the Y stand for?"

"You'll laugh."

"No. I promise."

"Yolanda. After my grandmother. The one who came from Sweden."

"I don't think it's funny. It's nice. A nice name. Yolanda." He smiled at her and began to outline her initials with small pieces of seashell and beach glass. A is for Allison. He thought he'd like to write a song, or maybe a poem about that.

"A is for Allison, Y for Yolanda. Put them together . . . while you sit on the verandah!" He spoke the last words with his arms outstretched, palms up, as though he were acknowledging applause.

Allison's laughter sounded different — almost like she was trying to make herself laugh. But when Nick looked at her, she flipped her hair away from her neck with the back of her hand in the usual way.

"Not totally awesome rhyming," he said, "but speaking of verandahs — I found out why Max was grouchy. And what it was he threw overboard. Or at least I think I did." He reached for a smooth white pebble, used it for a period after the A for Allison, and looked around for more.

"What?" Allison turned her head to look at him.

"One of the other ferry guys told a friend of my mother that he's been studying for his First Mate's papers. Carried his books everywhere in the bottom of the huge lunch pail, you know?"

She nodded.

"Just the day before the exam, after all that studying, he found out he didn't pass the medical. Guess that's why he was grouchy. Guess I would be, too, come to think of it."

"But what did he throw overboard?" asked Allison as she scooped up sand and let it trickle through her fingers.

"His books. He said he was so mad, he threw his books away."

They sat quietly for a few moments. The gulls' screeches were distant and muted, a slow-moving bee buzzed around an Oregon grape bush on the bank behind them and the water lapped over the sandstone. Allison rose onto her knees and peered into a tidal pool. She took a deep breath.

"How long will the moratorium last? On the logging?" asked Nick.

"I don't know. But my dad says he's had it."

"You mean he's going to quit?"

"I think so." Allison's voice was low and her head was bowed and he couldn't see her face because of the stream of hair.

"But not altogether? He's not going to quit altogether, Allison? That's not what people want."

"I guess not. But he says he's tired of it. Always the same old hassles. And he just — " she glanced up briefly and he saw tears pooled in her eyes " — just can't afford to." She stood quickly and walked along the beach a few steps with her back to him.

"Anyway." She turned to face him with her chin up and a defiant look on her face. "He's trying to sell the truck. And ... and ... so what if .... lots of people go bankrupt. It's not such a horrible thing. And he can get another job. Easy." She turned away again and clasped her hands to her cheeks.

Nick felt torn in two. He thought of the big blue and silver truck cab. The way it looked so proud and invincible standing there beside the flat pasture, making the sheep look like fluffy blobs. Would it still be able to flash its chrome mouldings and raise its black eyebrows without *McKeghnie Logging* on its door and the two thistles twined underneath? Where would it go? Would it be used for garbage, or toxic waste, or pipeline pipes? And what about the loggers? Where would they go? Could they get other jobs? He tried to imagine them carrying briefcases instead of chainsaws and sitting at desks instead of tramping around in forests.

Nick was overwhelmed with feelings. This seemed to be the time for a good "I" message, or something like that. He wished he had paid a little more attention to his mother when she talked about feelings. Expressing feelings, that's what she called it.

"Allison. I feel sad . . . about your father. And the truck. With his name on it . . . and the thistles . . . . Those thistles are so . . . so . . . ." *Why am I babbling about thistles? What do I really want to say?*

Allison had turned to face him again and her chin was trembling.

Nick tried again. "I feel mixed up." He talked to his feet. "Partly I'm glad they're going to stop logging. I really think we should save the trees. We need to find better ways to log and all that. But I feel sad about your father. And the loggers. About their jobs, and stuff. 'Cause they don't know how to do any other jobs, and anyway, jobs are tight right now, and, and all that . . . ." Nick paused for a second and glanced at her.

She seemed to be paying close attention. He looked away and then back at her face. "Allison. The thing I feel worst about is you. About you feeling bad. Because I like you a lot. More than any other girl in the world." He blurted the words out quickly, and Allison's face changed — her eyes got larger and her mouth got softer looking. Nick blushed and fanned his face with his hand as he turned away and said, "Geez, I wish my face wouldn't do that."

"I like you too, Nick. And that's why . . . because you're sort of shy . . . and you don't act, like, smart alecky . . . and . . . ." Her voice was close to his ear.

Suddenly the situation was too much for Nick to handle. He wanted to put his arms around Allison and kiss her and ask her to go out, but he knew he didn't have the nerve right then. One of these days, maybe, but not right then.

"It's like the spider webs in the fog," he said abruptly.

"Pardon?"

"You know. The spider webs are there all the time, but in the fog you see them better. I guess a lot of things are like that. It's easy not to see stuff you don't want to see. Like thinking your side of things is right and the other person . . . ." Nick trailed off.

"Yeah," said Allison. She was smiling.

She pointed to a small pool. "It's a whole world in miniature in there. Look. You can see the barnacles eating."

Nick leaned over beside her and the pool became as still and lifeless as a snapshot. They waited without moving, and gradually the snapshot turned into a silent movie. They watched wispy filaments dart out of the middle of small volcano-like barnacles. The narrow slits in the volcano tops opened and closed as the creatures shoved invisible bits of food into their mouths with their feet. Hairy hermit crabs crept along the rock bottom in their too-small borrowed snail shells, and brownish-green crabs no bigger than a baby's fingernail sidled along sideways in little bursts of activity. Bullheads swam among the weeds. The reflected light in the pool changed to bright red and mauve. Allison and Nick sat back against a log and watched the sunset.

Nick could smell Allison's faint soap smell and the sweet wine-like aroma of crushed berries. The salt-water and sea-animal smell of the ocean swirled around them. A squirrel chattered from the branches of a fir tree just behind them and Nick turned to chatter back.

"Chirt-chirt-chirt-chirt-chirt," he said. The squirrel darted down the tree and stared at them with black beady eyes, its tail flicking back and forth in small sharp movements.

"I didn't know you could speak squirrelese," said Allison. The squirrel scampered back up the tree.

Nick laughed. "Not much trick to it. They're so curious, they'll come to investigate any steady sound. You can get them real close just tapping two stones together."

Nick stood, picked up the medicine stick and offered it to Allison. "Here. I want you to have it."

"No." She pushed his hands lightly away. "You already gave me the spoon, and I'm going to keep it forever. My mother says it's old, but not really valuable, so it's okay if I keep it?"

Nick nodded. "Sure. I said you could, didn't I? I want you to keep it. And I want you to keep the medicine stick too. My dad would say it's okay to give it to you. He always says... what is it? 'Gifts are gifts. You can do anything you want with them.' It's unconditional."

"No. I want it to protect you. You saved my life, now this medicine stick will guard yours." She lifted the stick, stood in front of him and swayed back and forth as she chanted.

> *Creatures of the briny deep*
> *Spirits of the island*
> *Witches, trolls and leprechauns*
> *Please just step this way*
> *Gather all your spooky wits*
> *Bring along your magic kits*
> *Come and do some voodoo, voodoo, voodoo*
> *Just a touch of voodoo*
> *Keep all harm away*
> *Just a smidge of voodoo, voodoo, voodoo*
> *Make this stick look after Nick*
> *Protect him night and day.*

She placed the stick across his knees and knelt down beside him. Her face was close, and her hair brushed against his hand. His heart was acting strange, and he thought about being under a spell. He wanted to touch her, maybe lean forward and kiss her right now, instead of some other day.

"Whatcha doing?" Jonathan's voice was cheerful and loud behind them. Nick turned and looked along the path. There he was, waving a dead arbutus tree branch, followed closely by Stephanie.

"Allison. Hi." Stephanie bounced down onto the beach

and put her arm around Allison's waist. Jonathan sat with
a thud beside Nick, waving the branch in front of him in a
reckless way.

"Watch it with that thing. You nearly hit Allison," said
Nick irritably. Jonathan was about the last person he was
interested in having a conversation with right now. But Allison was being nice to her sister, so . . . .

"Mom says come on home. We're having a deegriefing."

"Debriefing," said Nick.

"What is that? Dee . . . ?" Jonathan held the branch
aloft in both hands and looked up at it.

"Debriefing. It means to talk about what happened.
And how everybody feels," said Nick.

"Well, anyway. Allison got saved. And Allison's whole
family, and even the cops, and the neighbours are coming," said Jonathan. "Escept Uncle Hayloft," he added.
"He can't come 'cause he's . . . ."

"I know," said Nick.

"I'm glad I won't have to spill anything on anybody's
clothes, now," said Allison. She looked at Nick over
Stephanie's head and winked.

"Right," said Nick. "Thomas Turner can drink his tea
in peace." He winked back.

Jonathan looked angrily from Nick to Allison. "What
are you guys talking about? Spilling stuff. What does that
mean? I know. You're talking code. Just so we can't understand. Aren't they?" he added, to Stephanie.

"I guess so," said Stephanie, and smiled up at her sister.

Allison held Nick's hand as they walked back home.

"What do you think The Timex Two should do next?"
she whispered.

"Um. Don't know. Are you . . . aren't you going back
to Vancouver? Or somewhere?"

"Yeah, yeah. We are. But then we're moving to
Nanaimo. My dad just decided today. So, I guess I'll see
you at school?"

"I guess." Nick felt tall and strong and balanced and happy as he walked with one hand holding Allison's and the other holding the medicine stick.

"Where is geek city?" said Jonathan. Nick laughed. One could always trust his little brother to break a mood. But he didn't really care.

"I don't know," said Stephanie. "Ask Allison. She's smart."

Smart and beautiful, thought Nick, and he turned his head to look into her blue eyes.

Elwood Miles

Marion Woodson has always loved the Gulf Islands, having lived on Gabriola Island for six years. She captures that love, magic and mystery in *The Amazon Influence*, her second book for young people. Marion's first book, *Mid's Summer . . . the Horse Race* (Pacific Edge Publishing, 1989), was nominated for the Manitoba Readers Choice Award. Writing lyrics to songs and skits for local folk festivals keeps the fun in life. Marion lives in Nanaimo, BC, and has five grandsons to share books with.